Wildflower Fever

A novel by

Regan Strater

Simple Man Press
Albuquerque, New Mexico

For information, contact: reganstrater@gmail.com

Published by
Simple Man Press
Albuquerque, New Mexico
All rights reserved.

Distributed globally by:
www.Lulu.com

Cover art and design by Cyd Riley, www.fireflystudiosart.com
Source image: South Texas scene from detail of a painting
by Violet Gibson Walker, circa early 1940s.

Printed in the United States of America
Library of Congress Cataloging-in-Publication
Data has been applied for.
Wildflower Fever by Regan Strater

ISBN 978-0-6151-6855-5

For the memory of

Lady Bird Johnson,
who inspired me to love
wildflowers and all of nature,

and

Louis Owens, my fiction writing professor and
thesis committee chair, who encouraged my writing
Wildflower Fever during graduate school at the
University of New Mexico, circa 1993-95.

That summer fields grew high. We had wildflower fever.
We had to lay down where they grew.
                    —10,000 Maniacs, Our Time in Eden

[P]eople don't change. They only stand more revealed.
                    —Charles Olson, The Maximus Poems

1

The week after Aunt Ivy's funeral I caught up on my only client's yard work at the well-tended estate on Windsor Avenue. It belonged to Dr. Moody's wife, Helen. Dr. Moody, the grandson of an early Texas philanthropist, had been dead for years, but Helen still liked being referred to as Dr. Moody's wife. It was early May 1990, and I had been working for her for three months, maintaining the lawn and tending her gardens, which she liked to keep on par with the others in her grand neighborhood known as Old West Austin. I had quit my copy-writing job at the ad agency after the New Year during what felt like the beginning of a midlife crisis, except I was only twenty-eight years old.

On my first morning back to work, Helen joined me outside, wearing a crisp yellow blouse, khaki skirt, and soiled tennis shoes. A wide brimmed flaxen hat shaded her face. Her perennial flower beds, which were filled with pastel yarrows and the indigo spires of gentian sage, had become overgrown and full of young weeds, mainly dandelion, milkweed, and Bermuda grass, which I hated most because of its deep roots. I was crouched near a grouping of herbs, struggling to get all the grass hidden beneath a canopy of fragrant spearmint plants, when she walked over to me.

"You know, David, I would do more of this myself if it weren't for my back." She had one hand on her hip and was attempting to dead-head the perennials—picking off the spent blossoms so more would bloom—with the other.

"Are you taking anything?"

"Just some pills Dr. Flahredy prescribed. He was a good friend to my husband, you know. I trust him completely, but I'm still afraid to take them. I don't even like to take an aspirin." She put her picking hand against the small of her back and stood up straight.

"Try taking them, just to see if they help." I scooted over to the bushy tarragon and oregano.

"Oh David, you're so right. I sometimes think my body is supposed to start giving out on me. I'm getting up there, you know. I'll be seventy-five in four months, September 6." She stopped tending the flowers and sat in a lawn chair, which creaked as she settled her soft body into it. She picked up a glass of ice-water, held it against her cheek for a moment, and then took a long drink.

"Are you having a birthday party?" I noticed the wheelbarrow handles needed painting and decided to paint all the tool handles the following week.

"My bridge club is meeting at my house that Saturday. Since I'll be hosting, I'm planning on something special. It'll only be a group of thirteen old women, but there will be plenty of good food. I'd love for you stop by, if only to have a piece of cake."

"I'd love to help you celebrate, Helen. Thanks for including me." As I was digging around the basil I noticed much of the lower foliage had been eaten by slugs.

"Of course, dear, bring a friend if you'd like." She took another drink of water. "I only wish that I could function like when I was sixty-five. Now *that's* a good age."

"Seventy-five's not that old and you look great. Besides, if you still did everything yourself I'd be unemployed."

"That's right, David." She nodded and laughed. "I'm helping the economy *and* doing you a favor . . . idle hands, you know."

"Yeah, there's no telling what I'd be doing." I laughed, not having a clue as to what I'd be doing, and continued weeding. "Helen, have you noticed any snails or slugs down here lately?"

"No, but I've seen their handiwork. I may have 'Slug Death' powder in the greenhouse."

I shuddered at hearing the name.

"I agree. Isn't that a horrible brand name?"

Mrs. Moody spoke in a lyrical drawl, genuine and empathetic. I imagined her voice was similar to that of Lady Bird Johnson. She hid a yawn by fanning at the gnats that buzzed near her face.

"I don't think we should use that stuff. I'll find something organic, maybe something that will just keep them away." I peeled off my cotton gloves, which had become slick black with dirt and the sap of freshly pulled weeds, and tossed them into the wheelbarrow.

I began shoveling crushed bark mulch around all the plants. The coarsely ground mixture smelled of pine trees. "You know, only the bottom of the plants have been eaten. I think we should let their little slugfest continue. They deserve some good food too." I turned to Mrs. Moody and smiled. "What do you think?"

"You're so right, David. I could never use all that basil if I lived to be a hundred." Wrinkles bunched below her turquoise eyes as she sat smiling, expressing the relief of a softhearted queen who had just pardoned someone sentenced to die. She sat quietly and watched a hummingbird feed on a red, fluted hibiscus blossom.

I removed the flower heads from the early blooming herbs to keep them from going to seed. The heat was forcing them to bloom too soon. As I pinched back the basil its anise scent reached my nose and made me think of Lexy's pesto. I picked a large bunch of leaf clusters to give to her.

"David, the sun's getting to me, I'm going in." Mrs. Moody picked up her empty glass from the lawn and adjusted her hat. "I'll see you on Friday, right?"

"Of course, it's payday." I looked up at her and smiled.

"Oh, David." She flopped her hand forward on a loose-skinned wrist and walked toward her house. "Have a pleasant afternoon."

"Thanks, you too."

I rinsed off the tools, got my bike out of the greenhouse and peddled home.

I filled a wine glass with water and ran a bath before stripping out of my sweaty t-shirt and shorts. I stepped into the hot water and sat, enjoying the familiar wet heat envelop my lower body. I lay back so the rising water would cover my body, its buoyant cushioning and warmth soothing my fatigued muscles. I took a large drink of water and set the base of the glass on my stomach, suctioning it against my skin as I arched my back up out of the water with a slight splash. I held the stem of the half-empty glass with one hand and ran a wet finger in circles along its rim with the other. The uneven shrill became a hollow tone that echoed in the small tiled bathroom. I closed my eyes and thought about what I was going to do with Aunt Ivy's house.

Aunt Ivy, my great-grandfather's youngest sister, had raised me after my parents were gone. Mom had died from leukemia when I was twelve, which was six months before my father was sentenced to 25-years-to-life in Huntsville for killing a man with whom he had worked at his accounting firm. It was a hunting incident. Dad claimed it was an accident, but his jury didn't believe him. Aunt Ivy shielded me from most news coverage, but I managed to read some of the newspaper articles at school. I didn't know who or what to believe.

Because I was already almost a teenager when everything happened, Aunt Ivy didn't really raise me. I just stayed with her until I went away to college. We lived in one of the few small houses in Alamo Heights, an old money part of San Antonio, but I never thought she was rich but rather just immune to the world.

She had been a young seventy-eight the day I moved in and looked like a full-color rendering on a vintage McCall's pattern, impeccable A-line skirt to her calves, the waist cinched. Pearls hung from her neck and were clipped against her ears. She seemed thrilled to have me come live with her, almost as if the tragedy surrounding my arrival were just a bothersome means to an end.

The day the attorney dropped me off at her house, I remember looking down at the uneven flagstone path, wanting it to stretch for miles. I eventually reached the wide wooden porch that was framed by a paint-chipped white lattice trellis through which blooming red roses twined.

Aunt Ivy had been standing inside the house behind the shadow of the screen door. As I approached, she pushed open the door and held a clutched hand just below her neck. She then hugged me for just an instant as if she feared hurting me. Tears clumped her lashes. She turned away and promptly led me into the kitchen where a plate of warm oatmeal cookies and iced lemonade waited, beads of moisture starting to run on the crystal pitcher. A crazed fly buzzed at the window bordered by a vine growing from a sweet potato tooth-picked in a jar. She poured a glass for me and started to say something, but instead she walked out of the room, her black pumps tapping across the faded linoleum tiles.

* * *

I lifted my hands out of the now tepid water and looked at my creased fingertips as drops of water fell from my hands. I flipped the tub's drain lever with my toe and remained lying there as the water level slowly dropped.

By the time the tub had finished draining I was almost dry. I got out and lay on my new Craftmatic bed. My head pounded as the remaining dampness of my naked body absorbed into the cool cotton sheets stretching over the bed that I had saved for months to buy, after studying the brochure I received by calling the toll-free number in one of Aunt Ivy's magazines. Because its mechanical parts were hidden beneath a boxed-in frame of oak veneer, it looked like a normal queen size bed when flat. I had known it would make me want to find reasons not to get up for days, tilting it up to read, level to sleep, up and down for slow motion sit-ups. I had wanted one ever since I saw Art Linkletter selling them on television when I was a kid, thinking they were being wasted on the old people in the commercial.

Ragged National Geographic magazines were scattered on the bedside table next to a crinkly Oreo package and a pitcher of warm Kool-Aid. Because she was still uncertain about my new bed, Abby slept next to it instead of on it, her reddish brown retriever's coat camouflaged against the hardwood floor.

My best friend Lexy came in through the front door without knocking. While I was still sprawled on the bed she blew past the bedroom door and stood beside me, hands on hips, smiling. Abby jumped up and ran to her. She sat at her feet, snout up and tail wagging. The sun streamed through sheer white curtains, its light dappled by the untamed wisteria vine outside.

"Good girl, Abigail. Aunt Lexy loves you too." She patted her on the head and then turned to me. "Expecting someone else?" She tossed the top sheet over my waist and grabbed an Oreo and sat beside me, sunglasses smoothing her straight hair behind her ears, crumbs jumping like fleas on the white sheets. I brushed them onto the floor where Abby licked at them, her tail slowing over the slight taste. She looked up but I only offered her a few strokes to her head and she fell again to the floor, stretching, her tail thumping to a stop.

"Want some pink stuff? I pointed to the Kool-Aid. "It's really yummy, Lex."

"Thanks, no." Lexy smiled and looked around the room as if she were seeing it for the first time. "What's with the junk food?"

"Come on, have some. Sure it's a little sweet but it has this fruity little finish." I smiled and picked up the plastic yellow pitcher and pulled the sheet to my chest.

Lexy looked great, even on a Saturday morning when she didn't have to. Her hair reached her shoulders and was black like mine but with a reddish tint. Her skin was unnaturally white for Texas in late spring. Ever since we were in college together, after she had read all the articles about how tanning caused premature wrinkling, she'd been addicted to sunscreen. She wore a black tank top over plaid madras shorts, and her arms and legs were lean and evenly muscled. She lay back on the bed next to me and sighed loudly as if her entire life were a bother. She rubbed her hair. "Can I borrow your bathroom? I've got an appointment with Mara in an hour and I can't have dirty hair. My water heater's busted."

"Doesn't she wash it before she cuts it?"

"Of course she washes it, but I don't want her to think I've got oily hair."

I pulled on a pair of sweat suit bottoms and followed her into the bathroom, looking briefly at myself in the mirror hanging above the dresser. I appeared thinner than I really was, and my three-day beard looked dark against my face, which had become tanned like my arms from so many mornings in Mrs. Moody's gardens. My hair was almost past my ears and I ruffled it with my hand. "Maybe you should make an appointment for me while you're there."

I followed Lexy into the bathroom, closed the toilet seat and sat while she leaned her head into the flow filling the basin. Her hair became weighted down by the water, and then suddenly buoyant.

"Mara's a little weird, but you'd like her." Lexy looked at me upside down, her voice now nasal as she lathered shampoo into her hair. She rinsed and then swirled a towel onto her head and squeezed, tightening it into place.

We walked back to my bedroom and she fell onto my bed and pressed the middle button on the controls. I heard the motor hum and watched the mattress snake into a prostrate S beneath her. She picked up a National Geographic, the one with a green death mask on the cover, "Jade, Stone of Heaven," and began to thumb through it, sipping from the diet Coke can she had brought with her.

I had known Lexy for ten years. We met as freshmen at a party in someone's dorm room. My best friend Michael, who had a class with her, introduced us. When I arrived at the party Michael pulled me aside, pointed toward Lexy and said, "You got to meet this Lexy, Dave. I can tell, she's going to want you." He clapped me on the shoulder, "Oh yes, she's going to want you bad." He laughed.

Lexy was standing near a group of guys, moving her body to a Dire Straights ballad, smiling, rocking her head to the beat. She looked over at Michael and me as soon as I arrived. She had a lit cigarette in one hand and a cup of straight tequila in the other. Her hair was in a short new wave cut, black and noticeably lustrous. I thought she looked interesting, attractive even. We talked, danced, even kissed a while. We both got drunk. She came on to me in a big way and I played along. After an hour she could barely stand up. I guided her back to her room where she passed out. I was later thankful that she had fallen asleep.

I didn't see her again that semester. In the spring we had an English class together. I hardly recognized her sitting at the back of the room. She wore her hair in a pageboy and had the fresh-scrubbed look of a third year sorority sister. She was definitely beautiful. It was hard for me to believe she was the same girl from the party. I hadn't changed my mind about not wanting to date her. She still intimidated me. I didn't know what it was about her that made me feel that way. I thought it could be because I really was attracted to her, or maybe because I wasn't. And stuff like that, girls and sex, always scared me.

Lexy tossed the magazine on the floor, sat up on the bed and drained her Coke. As if she had just remembered, she said, "Where were you last Sunday night? I came by around seven to see if you wanted to grab a bite at Chuy's and your door was locked."

"Sorry." I moved to the window and released the catch on the blinds. They fluttered down hard, slapping the sill. "I was in a funk and went out, sort of spontaneously."

"So where'd you go?"

"Cedar Door for a beer. I should've called you I know, but I thought I wanted to be alone." I sat on the bed next to her and put my head in my hands, which were damp with sweat. "It didn't help me feel better, though. I got really drunk and saw this graffiti on a wall in the bar's restroom that read: All I want out of life is beautiful lovers and immortality." I looked at Lexy as if hearing the line should affect her. I wanted it to affect her.

"Sooo?" she said slowly, staring at me, bobbing her head.

"So, well, I haven't had many beautiful lovers and I'm going to die." I grabbed a pillow off the bed, and while hugging it dropped to the floor and started petting Abby.

"You're not going to die," she said. "Well, not for fifty years at least." Lexy bent alongside the bed and held my face in her hands inches from her own. "Cheer up, David. Things could be worse, you've still got me."

Seeming to forget about her hair appointment, she picked up another magazine and studied a full-page photo of a killer whale closing in on a sea lion pup. "Say, when are you going to meet with your aunt's attorney again? Don't you need to sign more papers and do something with the house?" She leaned against the headboard. "You can tell me, David," she dropped the magazine and pretended to sound coy, "you didn't have some weird Harold and Maude thing going on with her, did you?"

I threw a pillow at her, tumbling the red and white terrycloth turban from her head, down onto the mattress where it lay like a melted peppermint candy.

After walking Lexy to the door I climbed back on my bed. For the first time, Abby jumped up and joined me. She lay beside me, rested her head on my calf, and sighed deeply as she closed her eyes. I watched her sleep, absorbed by her slow breathing and the fitful little movements of her dreams, and thought about Aunt Ivy and the family I once had.

Things hadn't really been that bad, not really, not before Mom got sick anyway. She had worked mornings at a neighborhood branch of the public library once I started kindergarten. My father had always been an accountant, a Certified Public Accountant, he'd remind us. We lived in a two-story brick house with a pool in a good neighborhood on the northwest side of San Antonio. We had lot of trees, which I started climbing when I was four, and a pool in the back yard. I didn't have grandparents or other close relatives besides Aunt Ivy, whom we rarely saw. Dad did tell me once to try to be extra nice to her though, because of an inheritance. But then he told me never mind because she'd probably leave it all to "Audubon, or some such crap." I never thought about it. After Mom died and Dad was gone, Aunt Ivy was all I had and not nearly as strange as Dad had made her out to be. It was easy being nice to her, without even trying. I guess I needed a new mom and, even though it had been decades since Karl had drowned, she needed another son.

When Mom was diagnosed with leukemia I knew she would die because this boy in my class at school, Tommy Baskin, had died from it two years before. She had to go to the hospital a lot, but she always got to come home after a few days. Dad started being so nice to her at that point, which was not how he usually was. He had always yelled about stuff she did or didn't do. He'd say things like, "Won't you *ever* learn to turn off the oven when you're done with it, you stupid bitch. For chrissakes, you'll burn the fucking house down yet." So his being nice to her made me uncomfortable. It made me know he was scared too.

The last time she was at Baptist Memorial I took her a plant Dad had bought for me to give her. It had rained on the way to the hospital, that light, intermittent rain so common to South Texas in the spring. I remember my clothes feeling warm and damp in Mom's room on the third floor. When the rain had let up, Dad went outside to smoke a cigarette while I finished visiting.

"I'm so sorry that things have been hard for you, David." She spoke in a soft, matter-of-fact voice. "But I want you to know that they'll get better. I know it's hard for you to believe sometimes, I know, but I know your father loves you." She smoothed the matted hair away from my forehead. Her hand felt softer and colder than usual, like it had been inside a rubber glove. "And always remember how much I love you."

Her voice was now weaker and sounded as if her mouth was dry. "I wish I could be home for you now."

"I know Mom, I love you too. Just get better, okay?" I bit the inside of my cheek.

"Everything's going to be okay." Her frosted brown hair had thinned to tufts like those on a worn, favorite doll. She picked at it with her fingers. "I must look pretty awful, huh?" She smiled, leaned forward, and kissed me. "Thank you so much for the beautiful plant. It makes me feel better just looking at it." She moved her head toward the gold foil wrapped pot with the green bow and smiled, but I could tell she wasn't feeling very well. "You should probably get going now. We'll see each other later."

I was suddenly aware of the smell of bland food and the sounds of carts being wheeled in the hallway. "Okay, I'll go find Dad." I kissed her on the cheek. "I love you."

I later missed someone telling me things would be okay. It didn't really matter if they turned out okay or not, but I liked having someone tell me they would. I thought it was sort of like people believing in a heaven, in that it wasn't important whether it existed or not, because no one really knew, but it was the believing that made them feel better. I began to believe a lot of things to make me feel better, like Dad would take care of me without someone there to make him.

Like Tommy Baskin, Mom died in the hospital during the night. Dad let me cry for a few days before telling me twelve was old enough to start behaving like a man. He did tell me Mom loved me very much, even more than she loved him, which didn't surprise either of us much. He said we'd have to get used to life without her, though it wouldn't be easy.

Dad brought the plant home from the hospital and I kept it in my room on the dresser by the window. The plastic tag sticking into the soil said it was a dieffenbachia, a dumb cane. It had large, dark green leaves spackled with white. I looked it up in one of Mom's plant books, which said its common name came from the fact that if you chewed on a leaf your tongue would swell up so much that you couldn't talk. I pampered that plant, following the tag's directions, watering only when dry and providing lots of indirect light.

Months later, after my dad was arrested and eventually taken away to prison for shooting that guy, I moved in with Aunt Ivy and took Mom's dumb cane with me. It had grown about a foot and Aunt Ivy helped me transplant it into a bigger pot so its roots wouldn't be so cramped. It looked content in its new home. I set it on the floor in my room and we lived together for a few weeks until it started to turn yellow and then died for no reason at all. And I just left it like that, in its pot in my room, and I cried for two weeks solid and no one even tried to make me stop.

* * *

It was already mid-afternoon when I drove over the Salado Creek bridge, turned left onto Broadway and worked my way through the stoplights of Alamo Heights to Gunther Avenue. Besides the grass being a little tall and weeds growing in the rose beds along the walk, Aunt Ivy's house looked the about the same—a simple clapboard bungalow, off-white with dark green trim. An unpruned privet hedge grew beneath the front windows.

The smell I remembered from the day I moved in with her fifteen years before, like the insides of old books and lemon scented furniture polish, hung in the still darkness. Even when I flipped on the light switch the room only glowed because Aunt Ivy hadn't believed in more than forty-watt bulbs and the white wood-slat blinds were closed tight. My high school graduation picture sat next to one of a young Aunt Ivy and a vase of dead roses on the piano. Seeing the white porcelain vase surprised me because I thought she hadn't been using the front of the house any more.

I grabbed a Pearl beer out of the refrigerator and twisted off its cold metal cap with the palm of my hand. Aunt Ivy had liked a beer now and then. She told me her doctor saw no harm in it, nor did I. The partial six-pack was all that remained, along with the balance of a dozen eggs, a stick of butter, a jar of Hershey's syrup and a box of baking soda, all huddled on the middle wire rack as if to keep each other company in the stark, bright whiteness.

I sipped from the beer as I walked down the hall toward Aunt Ivy's bedroom. I opened the door, which had been closed like always, and saw the unmade bed and imagined how things had happened. Her dying on those sheets, bright white and barely rumpled, her neighbor Lillian finding her, touching her neck, dialing 911, the ambulance coming without sirens. I squeezed my eyes shut for a moment and then pulled the cord to raise the blinds.

Going through her cedar-lined bedroom closet—the only place in the house that had been off-limits to me—I found boxes of letters, postcards and photos. A faded green postcard fell out of an album and onto the floor. It was from her older sister and postmarked April 8, 1924: "I am counting the days until next Sunday. We have had much rain so our crops look good. I can't wait to see baby Karl. Much love, Clara." On the other side of the card was an art nouveau relief of a field of wheat in front of a forest. It was rich with ordered curves and patterns. I returned the card to the album and took the last box from the top shelf. It was yellowed with age and smelled of mothballs. I lifted out a small ivory-colored gown, and round white pellets rained to the hardwood floor, tapping and rolling like tiny marbles. Wrapped in the gown was a black and white photograph of a little boy about a year old. Though I'd never seen the picture before, I knew it was of Aunt Ivy's son Karl. On the back of the frame was written in pencil: Karl Augustus Schumann, on the day of his baptism, February 27, 1924.

I looked closely at the photograph. The boy was wearing the gown that I had removed from the box along with white stockings and tiny sandals. He sat on a fluffy sheepskin covering an ornately carved table with his fingers interlocked on his lap. A linked silver or gold bracelet on his wrist had caught the photographer's flash and gleamed in the photo. His dark eyes were so full that only a thin outline of white showed. In place of a smile, he had a trusting expression on his face, contentment as if he'd just woken from a restful sleep. After a few minutes of staring into the photograph, I abruptly wrapped it back in the gown and put it away.

On Aunt Ivy's nightstand lay a box of tissues, a hand mirror, and a worn copy of Silent Spring, its dust jacket torn in places. Several cloth bookmarks extended out of the book. I placed it into the box of things I planned to take back to Austin.

I went out the kitchen door to the backyard, starting to feel more comfortable in confronting the task of handling Aunt Ivy's affairs. The screen door was in good repair and slapped tightly against the frame without a bounce. The house blocked the low sun, providing some relief. The flower and vegetable gardens were full of weeds, and the skeletons of the previous year's plants were covered with wild morning glory vines, their purple trumpet shaped blossoms wilted from the day's earlier heat.

I had always helped Aunt Ivy with her gardening, especially the grunt work, though she let me plant bulbs with her in the fall and pick vegetables and flowers during summer. She had a pronounced disdain for florist flowers, opting instead for bouquets of wildflowers, which she grew from seeds collected from her sister Clara's farm where she'd been born. After I went away to college she hired her cleaning lady's husband to take care of the yards. I missed helping her, but it was somehow easy to let others take care of her as I tried to begin a new life in Austin.

She never spoke Karl's name around me, not until almost a year after I moved in with her, in February just as the days were beginning to warm and the crocuses bloom. She had talked about what a meticulous gardener her late husband, my Uncle August, had been, and how he liked to bring Karl outdoors during his first spring and lay him on a blanket while he started working the soil and pruning "and so forth and so on." Aunt Ivy's memories always ended with that same phrase. She told me she had loved to look out of the kitchen window while doing the breakfast dishes and watch the two of them among the signs of life emerging in the gardens,

18

especially in the form of the green tapers that grew from the daffodil and tulip bulbs.

After pulling a few weeds from around her favorite Sweetheart rose bush, I walked into the detached garage. The wooden door latched upon closing with a clap of metal against metal, and the dusty room became dark and smelled stale from the trapped dampness of its dirt floor. My eyes adjusted to the low light glinting from the cracks around the doors. The lawn mower was pushed up against neatly stacked firewood and all the garden tools were hung from a row of hooks against one wall. Another wall was stacked high with cardboard boxes.

I started to open one labeled "David's Alamo Heights HS Stuff," and then shuddered, thankful I wasn't still fifteen, scared and alone. I had never made friends with the preppy kids of Alamo Heights High. I didn't even want to talk to them, so I avoided everyone at school except the teachers. Lying didn't become easy until several years later when I pledged the fraternity—the only place at college where it still mattered who your parents were. Yeah, Dad's an engineer for Exxon in Saudi, I told everyone, and Mom's a designer with Calvin Klein in New York. She lives with my stepfather and their two kids. Sure, they send me money, let me do what I want. Cool.

The only person in the frat to whom I told the truth was Michael. After hell week we both moved into the frat house. Our rooms were across the hall from each other. He turned me on to smoking weed and we spent a lot of time walking around Pease Park stoned, talking about life and not talking. He didn't care much about school and said attending class got in the way of his college experience. He got pretty wasted almost every night, partying with whoever was around. There was always somebody around, someone to stay up late with, someone to get high with, someone to knock off a six-pack and listen to albums with. We both knew the frat was fucked, but it was *our* fucked frat, comfortably, numbly there.

Sometimes Michael came along when I visited Aunt Ivy. She loved him. He gave her big hugs and told her she looked like a million bucks. Aunt Ivy once told Michael that she imagined Karl would have grown up to look like him, tall and good-looking with wavy blond hair, a wide grin and bright blue eyes with just a touch of the devil.

I had sorted through about five boxes before finding a large one that held a movie projector and several dozen reels of film, each in a small box the color of a school bus. I sat on the gravelly dirt floor and flipped through the boxes, reading the titles written in pencil in Mom's neat handwriting. I had never watched the home movies after I moved in with Aunt Ivy, though Mom had often played them for me after she found out she was ill. She had enjoyed pointing out what a "cute, happy little boy" I had been, as we watched me manically rip open Christmas presents or blow out a handful of candles on a birthday cake.

Though I couldn't find the screen, I carried the projector and a few reels into the house. I tacked a white sheet on the wall of Aunt Ivy's bedroom, which was the darkest room in the house, and closed the blinds. I turned on the power and the lamp cast a bright rectangle onto the sheet. I threaded the spliced end of the film into the projector and the motor pulled it in front of the lens, the smell of hot dust and machine oil filling the room. A soft clicking sound joined the drone of the motor as the film came out the other end and caught the uptake spool. I looked down at the empty box in my hands that had been labeled "David with Freckles, 1968." Full moons flickered on the soft colors that played over the sheet, then disappeared as an image came into focus.

I was about five, aimlessly running around our backyard. The lawn was brown from frost and I was wearing a red sweatshirt and blue pants and a pair of tan suede Hushpuppies. My black hair was a bowl of bangs and moved in a breeze.

Our Dalmatian, Freckles, ran over to me. She pushed me to the ground, and I was laughing when my father came into the frame. He was holding a red ball and waved it in front of Freckles who followed it with her eyes. He then threw it across the lawn and Freckles chased it and brought it back to him. Dad then gave the ball to me and I tossed it for Freckles and when she returned she tried to put the ball in my mouth. I was laughing and Dad was laughing and he took the ball from her mouth and threw it really far, and then he hugged me hard and ruffled my hair with his broad hand. And while he was hugging me Freckles ran over to us and jumped up and licked our faces.

Right then the film caught inside the projector and the image of Dad, Freckles and me huddled together froze and then vibrated on the sheet for a few moments before continuing. The rest of the film was overexposed and yellow but I let it play on, my attention no longer fixed on the flickering, translucent images.

And I remembered being there, in that yard of our home in the Oak Glen subdivision. I remembered the pyracantha shrubs, how Mom would point out the blue jays getting tipsy on the fermenting berries. I remembered the sour smell of those berries and the sound of the chains squeaking as Dad pushed me in the swing of my gym set. And I remembered feeling safe and happy. I knew that Dad hadn't just hugged me for the camera. I somehow felt as if Mom had filmed us so that I would be able to remember him like that.

The sheet became bright white as the clicking hum stopped, followed by the rhythmic sound of the film's end slapping against the projector in a tempo much too slow for my heart.

2

"I **don't feel guilty** about calling in sick." Lexy
adjusted the rearview mirror and checked her hair, pushing
stray strands behind her ears. It was Monday morning and
Lexy was riding with me to San Antonio for my initial
appointment with Aunt Ivy's attorney.

"Good for you." I always tried to make Lexy feel good
about her decisions, regardless of what I thought about them.
"I think companies expect employees to sometimes call in sick
when they're not. It's factored in as extra vacation time."

Lexy was the public relations manager for the LBJ
Presidential Library on the University of Texas campus. She
had lived in New York for three years after graduating from
college, working as an editorial assistant for New Woman,
before moving back to Austin.

"Right. And plus, ever since I started seeing that
nutritionist you told me about, I'm never *really* sick anymore.
I guess it all balances out." She rubbed at a week-old smudge
on my windshield from Abby's nose.

"Gail's an herbologist, not a nutritionist. She's sensitive
about the distinction."

"Right. I need to remember that, I wouldn't want to offend
her. Since I've been taking those extracts I never even get a
cold and my energy level has gone through the roof." She
poked at the canvas top of my Jeep.

"Great. I'm glad they've helped."

When we passed the Onion Creek Country Club exit I finally felt out of the city. I rolled down my window. Pastureland, dotted with cattle, live oak trees and cedar elm, lay on both sides of the interstate. I thought it would only be a matter of time before the sixty mile stretch between Austin and San Antonio was swallowed up into one huge city.

"So, anyway. You know I work really hard at my job, and I've already finished the initial planning for the fall fund raiser, so I think I deserve a longer weekend."

"Of course you do, baby." I reached over and patted her shoulder, mocking her. "You should call in sick every day this week, just to show them who's in charge." I smiled. Lexy pulled away from me and made a face.

I readjusted the rearview mirror and watched the navy blue Volvo tailgating me. In the front seat was an attractive couple around forty years old. The man driving was wearing a white button-down shirt and the woman had on a tie-dyed t-shirt. Two children bopped around in the back seat. The woman was talking to the windshield while the man stared blankly ahead, seemingly right into my rearview mirror. He nodded occasionally, as if he weren't really listening. Probably heading to Sea World, I decided. I tapped my brakes to piss him off. He passed me and sped out of focus.

I dropped Lexy off at the River Center Mall across from the Alamo so she could shop during my meeting. We had agreed to meet for lunch at La Mansión del Rio an hour later. I parked in a garage on Crockett near Bowie and walked across the street to a limestone office building that was dwarfed by slick granite skyscrapers on either side. It was merely late morning but the city's air was already becoming stale as the sun's heat began releasing the smell of new asphalt, garbage dumpsters and too many people. I took the elevator to the fourth floor.

Balding, middle-aged and dressed in a light gray suit pinstriped with navy, Friedreich Goetz stepped into the reception area carrying a large leather case. The thick salmon-colored carpet absorbed his footsteps as he walked toward me.

"Nice to see you again, Mr. Thorpe. Sorry, I mean David. No need to get up," he said, holding out his right hand. "We'll meet out here if it's okay with you. My office is particularly cluttered this morning." The handshake was long and overly friendly, a type which made me think the shaker wanted something from me. His too smooth hands ended in manicured nails. He nodded to his secretary who noiselessly left the room. We sat on the couch and he spread the contents of the case on the broad mahogany coffee table.

"Here's the last of the papers from Mrs. Schumann's estate along with the items from the safe deposit box at Alamo National." He handed me the bank's inventory: bonds, stock certificates, deeds to the house and farm, insurance papers, gold coins, a few rings and other jewelry. I shifted my weight in the overstuffed couch and my eyes blurred at all the papers Goetz was shuffling in front of me.

"All the savings and investment accounts have been changed to your name. Smart decision to stay with your aunt's portfolio. She was quite shrewd, investment wise. Clark Nelson at Merrill Lynch prepared this folder for you. It contains the most current statements on all the accounts. His card's inside. Call him anytime." Goetz leaned back into the sofa. "You're a lucky young man, Mr. Thorpe. Set for life, there's little doubt." His breath smelled of wintergreen mints and cigarette smoke.

I stifled a yawned and glanced at my watch. He gathered the files and stuffed them into the case.

"By the way, when I was going through your aunt's files I found this envelope containing papers that belonged to her husband. Looks like personal stuff, letters and such. I'm sure you'll want to go through it privately." He gestured with the envelope trying to catch my attention. "My father had been Mr. Schumann's attorney, you know. You might say I *inherited* your aunt as a client." He laughed slightly.

"I never knew Uncle August," I said as if I couldn't have cared less.

"No, I guess you couldn't have known him." Goetz looked

at the outside of the darkened manila envelope looped closed with a waxy red string. "Looks like he died in '56, long before you came along, my boy." He shoved the envelope into the leather case with the rest of the papers. We stood as he extended the case, which I took from him and held with both hands to avoid another handshake.

"If you have any questions, just give my secretary a call." He smiled. "I'd like for you to consider retaining me as your attorney, unless of course you have other plans. You never know when a man with your complicated affairs will need counsel." He smiled again, hopefully.

"Sure, Friedreich." I smiled, warming up to him, and extended my hand.

* * *

I met Lexy at the restaurant and we were seated at an outside table along the river walk. We had a view of the San Antonio River, which was merely a canal through the old mission city. Its cement banks forced it to meander among high-rise hotels, restaurants and shops, new paths dictated by the latest high-rise developments. The large cypress trees, clumps of banana trees and other subtropical vegetation softened the commercial nature of the perennial tourist attraction. A purplish pink gasoline sheen formed on the river's surface in the low wake of a tourist barge slowly motoring past our table.

"They drain the downtown part of the river each February." I said flatly. "It's so they can clean out all the stuff that ends up on the bottom."

"Really?" Lexy's voice matched my disinterest as she looked beyond me toward a young man in belted shorts and a black t-shirt who walked along the river. "What sort of stuff?"

"Could be anything. Sunglasses, trash, dead fish or other animals, assorted coins."

"Hmm. Can we go over there after lunch?" Lexy pointed to a cluster of boutiques on the other side of the river near an arched rock bridge. She smiled when I nodded and then pointed toward a woman in a short red lamé dress. "Can you believe the things some people will wear in public during the day? I mean, really."

Lexy began to open a shopping bag. "Let me show you what I bought." She peered into the large, colorful bag. "Of course, some things were more expensive because of the location, but I found some real cute tops which had been marked down at Saks."

"You can show me later. Look, the table's not wiped clean yet. You'll get your new shirts dirty." I looked around for our waiter.

"You're right." Lexy put the bag on one of the two empty chairs at our table. "I could really use a margarita. The service here seems pretty lame. Why'd you pick this place?"

"I don't know." I looked around again. "I guess it's because the tables aren't packed in like most of the other cafes down here."

"Here comes our waiter, I think. Gosh, he's really cute," Lexy whispered to me, smiling. "Hola, babeee."

"Shhh. He's going to hear you."

"So what if he does?" Lexy shot back.

"Hi, I'm Marcos. May I get you two something from the bar while you decide?" He wiped off our table and laid out two place settings.

Lexy folded the menu she had swiped from the host's stand and tossed her hair back, smiling. "Yes, but you can take our entire order now. We've had enough time to decide."

I smiled at Lexy, admiring her confidence and control.

"We'd like two margaritas, on the rocks without salt, and two glasses of ice water. Then, we'd like to start with the ceviche and the guacamole plate and then . . . ." While Lexy continued rattling off the order she selected for us, I watched our waiter trying to keep up on his note pad. He was Latino, fit, and his long black hair was pulled back into a short ponytail. I thought he was certainly good-looking enough to be a La Mansión waiter, but he didn't seem to have that professional waiter attitude. I imagined him to be a grad student at Trinity or St. Mary's in architecture, or botany perhaps.

He turned to me and smiled as I handed him my menu. In a few minutes he returned with our margaritas and water. I took a long drink of water and Lexy sipped her margarita.

"Mmmm, David. This is really good. Taste yours." She took another sip. "Go ahead, taste it, it's not a mix. Taste it." Lexy unfolded a white linen napkin and placed it on her lap.

"I will, Lexy. Calm down."

"Oh, David, come on. Let me be excited. Look," she pushed her hair behind her ears, "I'm having a great day. I called in sick, I got to go shopping at Lord & Taylor and Saks, I'm having a great margarita in this beautiful tropical setting— and we have a cute waiter. I think I'm entitled."

"Of course, Lex. I'm sorry. Maybe I'm just envious of your mood."

"I know, I'm sorry." She reached out her hand to cover mine. "I keep forgetting you're still mourning your aunt. You'll feel better soon. Have some of that margarita," she said and winked at me, which made me smile.

Our waiter brought us the ceviche and guacamole plus a basket of corn tortilla chips and a small bowl of green salsa. Lexy pulled out a brown bottle labeled in calligraphy, unscrewed its dropper and squeezed a stream of amber drops in the water remaining in her glass.

"What's that one for?" I dipped a chip into the salsa, which had been warmed and tasted of tomatillo, onion and jalapeño.

"It's an echinacea-astralagus tincture, good for the immune system." Lexy drank all of her water and then dipped a chip into the chunky guacamole. Marcos stopped at our table and refilled our water glasses.

"Geez, Lex. You *are* an herbal convert."

"This place is really nice, David. Thanks for bringing me here."

"Sure, of course. Who else would I bring?" I smiled. "How's Jack?"

"Oh, you know, same old thing. He works a lot, which is okay because so do I . . . ."

"Just not today." I smiled at Lexy.

"Just not today. But I deserve it. Now don't get me started."

"Sorry. So how are things going with you two?"

"Everything's fine. I really think Jack's good for me, though not always terribly exciting. I just wish he wasn't so young."

"How old is he again?"

"Don't remind me." She rolled her eyes. "Twenty-three."

"That's not *that* young. Besides, don't look for things to go wrong this time."

"I know, I know. He does make me really happy. I was so tired of being alone. Did you realize it's been almost a year since Nick and I broke up?

"Wow, a whole year." It seemed longer but I didn't point it out. "I know that was rough."

"Enough about my love life. I've held back long enough, but I'm just dying to know—how did your meeting go? How rich are you?" She took a long drink of her margarita but kept her brown eyes focused on me.

I laughed. "It's not that simple. It wasn't like the guy handed me an oversized check and sent me on my way like a sweepstakes winner."

"I know, I know, but . . . so, tell me about it."

"Basically, Aunt Ivy's attorney is an okay guy. I hated being there, you know, so I didn't ask a lot of questions. He handed me a list of stuff she had in a bank safety deposit box, gave me account statements with her broker, and . . . ."

"Your aunt had a broker?"

"Yeah, so? You knew she had money."

"It just seems weird, I don't know. So, okay then, approximately, how much? Over fifty thousand? A hundred?"

I was smiling at Lexy when Marcos stopped again at our table. "Your entrees will be right out. Would you like anything else?" He smiled at me for a protracted moment, in a way that made me feel he wasn't merely being polite, and then he turned toward Lexy. We both shook our heads and he walked away. I felt like asking him if he would like to join us for lunch but realized how absurd that would be.

"So, where was I, David? More than two hundred thousand?"

"Yeah, Lexy, it's more than that." My tongue was burning from the salsa so I took a drink of water, slurping a piece of ice into my mouth. "Quite a bit more, actually," I mumbled, looking at Lexy who had a piece of wet fish speared on a cocktail fork poised in front of her mouth.

"No way, David." Lexy's mouth dropped open even wider and she set the fork with the ceviche on it down.

"I really don't know the exact figures because there's a lot of property involved. And I didn't even look at the account statements," I lied. "But, yeah, it's a lot of money. Much more than I thought."

"That's incredible David, I had no idea." Lexy sipped from her margarita and then smiled. "Maybe Jack won't pan out after all, and you'll come to your senses and fall madly in love with me. And we'll both be rich, and live happily ever after." We both laughed and I glanced toward the sluggish gray-green river, which appeared even more sad and polluted than before.

Marcos passed by our table and Lexy motioned him over. He nodded to the people who were being seated at a table nearby and walked over to Lexy and me. She beamed at him. "We'd like to order something else if we could."

"Certainly, what would you like?" He looked at me again with the same intent, lingering smile.

"A bottle of your best champagne." Lexy looked over at me, giddy.

"Wonderful, we have several fine ones from which to choose. Let's see, we currently have Pelo Negro, Domaine Chanterlin, and this Italian sparkling wine called Amor Dolce, and of course, we have Dom Peri—"

"That, we'll have that. We're celebrating." Lexy's enthusiasm began to attract the attention of the foursome at the next table and suddenly I felt even more self-conscious. The waiter smiled at Lexy and then turned to me briefly, still smiling, but now with a questioning look in his eyes. I looked down at my plate, and the guacamole and ceviche no longer appeared appetizing. As the young man leaned forward to take away my empty margarita glass his cream-colored jacket hung open in front of me, releasing the musky aroma of an expensive cologne combined with the masculine scent of his body. I closed my eyes for a second and when I opened them he was gone, and I felt so alone.

Lexy cocked her head and smiled. "You're paying, right?"

"Of course, Lexy. I'll always be paying."

* * *

We headed out of downtown by driving up Broadway, past Incarnate Word College and into Alamo Heights, and turned onto Austin Highway just before the McNay Art Institute. During lunch Lexy had agreed to our stopping at Sunset Memorial Gardens, the cemetery where Aunt Ivy was buried, on the way home.

I drove through the opened wrought iron gates, which looked like they belonged on the grounds of a gothic estate. I parked the car and then led Lexy across the lawn, which was as carefully trimmed as a golf course. Lexy followed as I zigzagged among the ground-level headstones trying to remember the spot. They were all the same, a sea of gray granite slabs, with a smattering of dwarf evergreens. I soon spotted a low mound of black earth behind a triangle-shaped pine. As Lexy and I walked toward the grave I noticed how fresh the air smelled, like a late afternoon rainstorm was approaching. A slight breeze dispersed the scent of junipers. We sat on a small cement bench near the foot of Aunt Ivy's grave.

After about ten minutes my hands became suddenly cold and I couldn't shake the feeling that Sunset Memorial wasn't the right place for Aunt Ivy's remains. I thought she would not have liked that there were no real trees around to attract more birds, or that everything was so perfectly kept. But of course, she knew she would end up there someday, next to her husband.

I felt Lexy must have wanted to leave but she remained silently by my side. A mockingbird landed near Uncle August's headstone. It stepped around and stuck its beak into the grass a few times before Lexy shifted her leg and it flew away. The bird's white-gray plumage became quickly hidden against the overcast sky.

It felt cooler as the wind picked up. I put my arm around Lexy and held her slightly. The granite bench, still warm from the earlier sun, felt good against my legs.

I remembered the first time I had come to Sunset Memorial, when I was fourteen and living with Aunt Ivy. It had been the day after the first time she and I went to her family's farm, which then belonged to her sister, Clara. Though the cemetery was less than two miles from our house, we never visited together or brought flowers for Uncle August. I had told Aunt Ivy I was going for a bike ride around the neighborhood. Having just found out that Karl was buried on the farm where he had drowned, I had been curious to see where his father was buried. The cemetery attendant had referred to a directory of the dead before pointing me toward Uncle August's grave.

When I reached the spot I read the marker: Augustus Ivan Schumann / Born, Berlin, Germany 1892 / Died, San Antonio, Texas, 1956. Not understanding the ways of cemeteries, I had been startled by the headstone to the right: Ivy Krueger Schumann / Born Guadalupe County 1902. It was as if she were partly dead, and I became angry that a stone already had been engraved for her. Green-brown moss patches lined the words carved in the polished granite, and an empty flower receptacle had sat in front of Uncle August's marker.

Lexy shifted her weight against my body and lifted her head from my shoulder. I rubbed her back a little and we stood to leave. I hugged her as we began walking toward the car and whispered "thank you" into her humidity curled hair.

"Do you mind if I drive around New Braunfels awhile before continuing on?" I gave in to the weather and rolled up my window, cutting myself off from the smell of Sudan grass freshly cut for hay.

"Whatever you want is fine, David. I'm just so tired from the champagne." She closed her eyes again and leaned her head against the window, which was becoming spotted with tiny raindrops. I turned onto Walnut Avenue and headed downtown.

Aunt Ivy and I had spent a lot of time in New Braunfels. Most people who lived there usually drove to San Antonio to shop, but Aunt Ivy, who did live in the big city, came to New Braunfels. She said the people suited her. I drove downtown and made several passes around the old white gazebo, which had been handcrafted by German immigrants generations before. I remembered how all the shops had been decorated with cedar boughs and red ribbons six months earlier, when I had shopped for a Christmas present for Aunt Ivy. I had selected a silk scarf from Bruner's, which had always been one of her favorite stores.

I stayed with her for the last time that Christmas. She had just turned ninety and we celebrated her birthday by going out to lunch at Arthur's on Broadway. As I had each year since I moved out ten years earlier, I spent a whole week with her during the holidays. Everything was the same as in previous years—the tree ornaments, the Christmas dinner, the records on the phonograph playing carols.

The week after New Year's she called to thank me again for the scarf, and to tell me that she had decided to close off the front of her house because it cost too much to heat. She then invited me over for lunch the following Saturday, the day the cleaning ladies were to arrive.

Aunt Ivy was preparing lunch and I was sitting on the sun porch watching television while the women cleaned the front two bedrooms, as well as the living room and the dining room, as if their contents were to be shipped to a museum. After she had checked on the housekeepers' progress, Aunt Ivy told me she had given up the piano. I knew that she didn't mean playing—she'd given that up years before—but rather her *re*creation of playing. It had startled me the first time I saw her doing it a couple of years earlier. Her posture had been perfect and her closed mouth smile ethereal. She hadn't known I was watching. She was sitting at the piano, sheet music open to a dense black score of continual sixteenth notes. Her hands were poised on the keyboard, her eyes closed. I imagined her reliving a time when her fingers could fly over the keys, hitting every sharp and flat without exception, the andante perfectly andante and the allegro never merely allegretto. But that day she did not make a sound by actually plucking a key. Her stiff hands had since grown tired of even the primitive maneuvers of the gardener she had become.

Once the cleaning ladies had left I turned off the TV and went into the kitchen and poured iced tea and finished setting the table. I was waiting for Aunt Ivy to return from her inspection of the cleaned rooms. After having taken twice as long as I thought she should have, she passed through the dining room doorway and into the kitchen, touching her hair on one side, her knee-length blue linen dress wrinkled and longer than I had remembered.

I pointed out that she had forgotten to turn off the light in the dining room, and I turned to put a saucer of lemon wedges on the table for our tea.

She stepped back into the dining room, flipped the switch and closed the door. And with a single slow movement, her foot pushed a folded rug into the gap beneath the door.

"Do you know what, David?" Her brow was lined and she touched her hair again and then pointed to the sealed off rooms. "It looks like no one ever lived in that house. Like no one ever even lived there. But I know we did, didn't we Karl?" Her hands held the empty vase from the piano and she smiled. "Of course we did. I'm being foolish today, David, just plain foolish."

She set the white porcelain vase on the table and commented how especially beautiful it always looked filled with bluebonnets from the farm. Her blank expression matched that of the vase and I wanted to brighten both, but it was early January and wildflower season was still three months away.

After helping bring the food to the table she sat in her

usual chair across from me near the stove. She served us both and then placed her hands on her lap. The steam from the potatoes and asparagus obscured her face. I began to eat, and my fork's tapping my plate became the only sound in the house. Aunt Ivy continued to sit there, still, looking through me and into a whole other space altogether.

I pulled into the parking lot at Lexy's apartment building off Enfield Avenue. The rain had stopped but drops were still rolling off the leaves of the towering pecan trees on both sides of the building. I turned off the car and nudged Lexy. She resisted my efforts at waking her.

"Geez, Lex, you were really out. We're home. I've got to get going, Abby's waiting for her walk."

Lexy yawned. "Thanks again for lunch and everything. Give Abby a hug for me." She leaned over and kissed me on the cheek.

"Have fun at work tomorrow."

"Ugh." Lexy smiled. "Have a good walk. Stay dry."

She slammed the car door and I watched her walk toward her building, her sandals clapping against the wet sidewalk. "Yeah, a lot more, Lex," I whispered to myself and shook my head, thinking about the money, "five and a half million more." I moved the gearshift into first and slowly drove home to Abby.

3

When I first got to Mrs. Moody's house I laid out the gardening tools across saw-horses for painting. I had previously prepared each tool handle, progressively using finer grades of sand paper, when Helen slid open a glass door and shuffled onto her patio in beige, suede house slippers and a yellow silk robe that reached her ankles.

"Hello, David." Mrs. Moody surveyed the tools. "It looks like you've been here a while. I took one of those pain pills late last night and it just plain knocked me out."

"But did it help your back?" I wiped each handle clean with a soft rag.

"Yes, I believe it did. I guess I should keep taking them." She sat down at the patio table near large terra cotta pots of bougainvilleas, their arched branches filled with papery red blossoms.

"Sure, I would, as long as they're helping." I began applying a coat of primer and after a few minutes looked up at Mrs. Moody. "So what are you going to do today, Helen?"

"Oh, I don't know. I still feel so tired." She covered her mouth with her hand and leaned back into the padded chair.

"Maybe you should only take half of one of those pills." I finished applying the white enamel paint.

"I don't think it's the pills. I've been a little blue lately, but I'm feeling better today. Maybe I just needed that deep sleep." She crossed her legs, exposing a stubbly white calf.

"Why don't you get all dressed up and go shopping with one of your friends. You could start with a long lunch in the Driskill's dining room. I bet you haven't been there since the hotel was renovated."

"You're right, I haven't. That sounds like a fine idea, David. I'll call Elaine Jacoby. I owe her a lunch." She covered her exposed leg and sat up straight. "Looks like you've about finished here?"

"Yeah, I'm almost ready to take off." I cleaned the paintbrush in a glass jar filled with thinner, enjoying the smell of the fumes.

"Would you like to join me for a cup of coffee before you leave? I have a blueberry muffin with your name on it."

"Sounds yummy, but I can't stay. I'm meeting my friend Michael in half an hour." I flicked off the excess thinner against a drop cloth. "We're biking out to Laguna Gloria, and then maybe on to Mount Bonnell."

She glanced at the mid-morning sun overhead. "You've certainly picked a nice day for it. There's not a cloud in the sky."

"Yeah, it'll be hot, though, but I like to sweat. It makes me feel more organic or something." I smiled at her.

"Oh David, you're such a character." She began to walk back into the house, but stopped and turned toward me. "If the mountain laurel pods are dry enough up on Mt. Bonnell, would you mind bringing a few back for me? I think we should start some trees by seed. It will be an adventure."

"A *long-term* adventure," I said as I thought about the slow-growing, broad-leafed evergreens that grew wild, west of the city.

"One has to be optimistic and patient, David. There's just something special about growing a tree from a seed."

When I got home, Michael was already there, playing Frisbee with Abby in the backyard. I wheeled my bike through the front gate. Abby ran over and nosed me in the crotch. I knelt down and ruffled her thick coat and looked up at Michael, who was standing above me in well-worn khaki shorts and a faded blue t-shirt, his eyes the color of the Caribbean Sea. "You're early."

"Well, you know." He pointed to his bare wrist.

"Yeah, Abby's sure glad you're watchless."

"No, I'm *timeless*." He smiled.

"Clever." I tugged the purple, tooth-marked Frisbee out of her mouth and flung it across the yard. "I'm going to change. I'll be right out."

"Take your time." Abby had returned and was sitting in front of Michael, the Frisbee clutched between her teeth, her eyes daring him to take it away.

Michael and I reached the grounds of Laguna Gloria Art Museum by noon. The old estate sat on a large peninsula formed by Lake Austin and one of its inland canals. It had become a museum years before, after its owners had died and their heirs created a foundation to maintain the family's art collection. I'd only been through the museum one years before, but I liked the place because of the labyrinthine trails that wound through the grounds. They were bordered by huge oak trees that had been professionally pruned and tended for almost a hundred years. The native vegetation, a blend of shrubby trees and perennials, was interspersed with plants and trees cultivated to provide color during different seasons. The pale pink and apricot colors of the azaleas near the museum building had just about played out.

Michael and I racked our bikes and walked through the black iron gates and into the cool, green sanctuary. The red cinder of the paths crunched under our steps as we headed down the west trail, the one which traced the lake's edge though a thicket of oaks and shrubbery. The scent of a few lingering magnolia blossoms caught my attention as we began our hike.

"This was a good idea, David. I miss being by a lake during summer." Michael took in a deep breath. Though he had grown up in Dallas, his family owned a cabin on Lake Tyler in the Piney Woods. From what Michael had told me through the years, it sounded like heaven.

"Yeah, it's cooler here. Seems like there's always a breeze off the water."

Michael looked around. "I can't believe there's no one here." "It's usually dead like this. I don't know why more people don't come out." A short distance from shore a small motorboat maneuvered at no-wake speed up the small channel, heading out to the lake's open water. It was an aluminum skiff, about fourteen feet long. An older man of about sixty sat in the rear of the boat, hand-steering the small Evinrude outboard motor. His week's growth of beard matched his gray hair, which tousled in the slight wind. Every time I saw a man around that age, I thought of my father. Sometimes I imagined that the man was my father. That he was out of prison, that he was found innocent and that he had written me through the years. And I would wonder why he didn't steer his skiff over to Michael and me and offer to take us for a ride.

"You want to head over to Mt. Bonnell?" Michael asked.

"Not yet. I'd like to walk around here for a while, maybe climb a tree."

"You still do that?" Michael combed through his hair with his fingers.

"Yeah, but I don't do it at home. What would the neighbors think?"

"Okay, let's do it. Go ahead, pick a tree." Michael walked ahead of me.

"Hold your horses. It's got to be a good one. Let's keep walking."

We followed the trail as it curved east, away from the lake, and the sounds of the small waves lapping at the sandy shore faded along with the breeze. Within minutes I'd spotted the perfect climbing tree. I grabbed onto a low limb of the sprawling live oak and pulled myself into a sitting position near the trunk's first junction. Michael squeezed a drink from his water bottle and followed my lead. The old tree's bark was clean from the early summer rains and its leaves were a waxy deep green. I continued climbing until I was about ten feet above the ground and settled onto a thick horizontal limb. Michael found a similar perch a couple of feet below.

"Lexy called me yesterday. She's worried about you. She thinks you're still depressed about Aunt Ivy."

"Lexy loves to worry." I peered through the branches trying to get a better view of the water, looking for the skiff.

"I tried to explain that you're entitled to be depressed for a while, but you know Lexy, she thinks she knows what's best for everyone." Michael leaned against the limb supporting his back.

"I know."

"She means well, but sometimes she can go overboard with her mothering. She must have some Cancer lurking in her chart." Michael was a casual student of astrology, meaning that he'd read a few books. "That Cancerian energy is very maternal, very tied to the moon. You know, *la luna*, Mother Mooooon," Michael howled.

"Yeah, I guess so. Regardless, I cut her a lot of slack. I kind of like her smother love sometimes. She was my only connection here, you know, after you moved to Houston." I looked downed at Michael. "When she wasn't seriously dating someone, we did everything together. I think she was relieved when you moved back, so that I had another friend to dilute my time."

Michael laughed.

I glanced toward the canal, where the boat had been. "How're your parents?"

"Okay, I guess. I haven't spoken to them lately. They've pretty much left me alone since I told them I was gay."

"Is it bad?" I climbed to a higher limb and noticed the mossy scent of the lake in the breeze.

"Not really. I think they try, but it doesn't come natural for them. They call once a month or so. In a way, it's great. They don't bug me much about anything. I guess they figure since grandchildren are out of the picture now, why bother?"

"Do they still send you money?"

"Yeah." He answered sheepishly. "They don't think I can support myself with my art or the framing work at the gallery, so I cash the check each month and it keeps all of us happy." He laughed and then hung upside down from the branch on which he'd been sitting. His shirt fell to cover his head, revealing a flat abdomen covered with a thick mat of dark blond hair. He moved the shirt from his face and looked up and me. "I don't really need the money, but I think sending it makes them feel less guilty about not visiting anymore."

"So they didn't come to Houston either?"

"Not once in six years." He pulled himself back to a sitting position on the branch. "I like being up here. See the sailboats?" Michael pointed toward the lake.

"Yeah, it's a great tree." I leaned back against a thick branch.

"I can't wait for you to see my latest work."

"What's it look like?"

"It's made entirely out of copper, but since I'm considering it nonrepresentational, it sort of hard for me to describe, especially since it's not finished. But I think it's going to turn out pretty cool. I want it to produce certain sounds when air passes through it. I'm having this musician guy from the San Antonio Symphony help me tune the openings to a pentatonic scale."

"Sounds pretty cool." I heard the sound of a decelerating motorboat, looked toward the lake, but saw only choppy water. "Who's it for?"

"This woman named Missie Gordon commissioned it. Her husband's in the 'awl bidness in *You*ston,' as she would say. I'm meeting her again tomorrow at the installation site at their summer place out on Lake Travis." Michael climbed to a higher branch closer to me.

"Sounds like a deep-pocket client. I'd imagine they're the best kind." The wind picked up and the higher branches started to move.

"No kidding. By the way, I was telling Lexy about the piece the other day, and out of the blue she suggested that Mrs. Moody might be interested in being a patron for me."

"Helen?"

"Well, she didn't mention her by name but said something like, 'you should ask David,' but then acted sort of secretive, which seemed weird. Anyway, I just thought she meant . . . ."

"I know what she was getting at. She wanted you to ask *me* to underwrite your work."

"You?" Michael was hanging upside down again, the limb lodged beneath his bent legs.

"Yeah, me. She wants me to be more thrilled about it, but . . . well, you know how she went with me to San Antonio when I met with Aunt Ivy's attorney?"

"Yeah." The rough bark pulled at the skin on Michael's legs, bits of bark flaking off and falling to the ground.

"Well, it turns out Aunt Ivy left me everything, and now I'm technically a multimillionaire. Go figure."

At that moment Michael's legs became dislodged from the branch and he fell, landing on the bark mulch covering the ground. I scrambled down the tree and sat by his side. He lay on his back, eyes wide, and began to cough.

"Man, are you okay?"

"Fuck. I think I got the wind knocked out of me." He started to get up, coughing.

"No, don't." I held him down. "You might've hurt something. Do you feel any pain anywhere?"

Michael tried to laughed and winced. "Of course I feel pain, you fucker, I just fell from a fucking tree."

"Where does it hurt?"

"Everywhere, but I think it's mostly my ankle." He tried rotating his left foot. "Ahhhh." He squeezed his eyes shut, grimacing. "I don't think I'm going to be able to ride home."

I helped him to his feet. "Here, put your arm around me for balance." I guided his arm around my neck. "Let's just get you back to the museum. I'll ride home and bring back the Jeep."

"Sounds like a plan."

We began walking toward the parking lot, hobbling along like mismatched partners in a three-legged race.

"Hey, David."

"Yeah, what?"

"You weren't kidding about those millions, were you?"

When I returned an hour later, Michael was sitting on a green-veined marble bench, talking to an attractive man in his early forties who wore khaki pants and a seersucker blazer over a white shirt.

Michael looked up as I approached them. "Oh, hey David. This is Stephen Greene."

We shook hands. "How's it going?" I looked at Michael and squinted.

"Quite well, thank you. And you?" He smiled at me, showing perfect, overly white teeth.

"Stephen volunteers here once a month." Michael stood up, shifting his weight to one side. "He owns a gallery in that new building near Second Street, you know, Congress Avenue Plaza."

"Great. Well, it's been nice meeting you." I turned to Michael. "So, I guess we can go now."

Stephen handed a business card to Michael. "Call me next week. I'd love to see your work."

I secured Michael's bike on my roof rack and we began driving back to town. "How's your ankle?"

"It's still tender, but it'll be fine. He reached down and rubbed his injury. "I'll ice it when we get home. Hey, why don't you hang out at my place? We can share a joint and have a beer or two. I'm sure it'll take my mind off the pain." He flashed a sly smile at me.

"Sounds good." I turned on the radio.

Michael held his arm out the Jeep's window as if to catch the wind, pulled it back in, and then began manually rotating his ankle. "I'm excited about meeting that guy, Stephen. This might be a big break for me. I mean, you know, it's a tony downtown gallery. If, of course, he likes my stuff."

"Oh, I have a feeling he'll like your stuff all right."

"What's that supposed to mean?"

"Nothing, I'm kidding. Well, it just seemed like he was interested in you for more than just your art."

"You think? Really? I'm just hoping he'll give me a job so I can get away from the framing work. I'd be good at schmoozing customers in a nice gallery, don't you think?"

"Yeah," I replied, feigning a yawn. I didn't like the thought of Michael working in the new gallery, believing Stephen would make him work long hours and take him away from me. "You'd need a better wardrobe, though. Probably a suit. And maybe a haircut."

"We'll see. It'll probably amount to nothing." Michael stretched his neck, moving it from side to side and back and forth. "I'm with Lexy, David. I can't believe you're not more excited about your big inheritance. What the hell are you going to do with all that money?"

"Spend it, I guess. Haven't thought much about how, but you'll be the first to know."

A week later I was laying a flagstone patio in my backyard. Abby was lying on the lawn near me, gnawing on the knob end of a new rawhide bone. It was early afternoon and I noticed how hot it was getting. I decided to drive up to Mount Bonnell to get the mountain laurel seeds for Mrs. Moody.

I parked off the road near the million-dollar homes. The air was heavy with humidity and the sky was blue except for an occasional wisp of clouds. A slight breeze cooled my sweaty body as I started up the long stretch of steps through the cedar, mountain laurel, and scrub oak woods. Halfway to the top I stopped to tie my shoelace. I broke off a tiny cedar branch, crushed the foliage in my hand and held it to my face. Its fragrant scent reminded me of first moving to Austin and my hope for a new beginning. I crumpled the branch into my shorts pocket and continued to the top of the bluff. I found my favorite clearing and sat on the warm gray slate. The view never failed me with its wide strip of shimmering lake and rolling green hills beyond. A lone boat pulled a water-skier, splitting the lake with its wake a half mile below. At that moment I decided I wanted my ashes scattered on Mt. Bonnell when I died. Over the cliff on a clear spring day, dusting the purple mountain laurel blossoms, settling into the craggy rock, possibly blowing all the way down to the lake.

Right after I graduated from college, six years earlier, Michael and I had come to Mt. Bonnell for sunset like we'd done so often. He'd called me at work and said we should go. The evenings had been unusually cool, so no one was up there. He'd brought a six-pack and it was comfortably familiar.

"So who's Lexy sleeping with now?" Michael popped a top and handed me the can, spilling a little beer.

"She says nobody and I believe her. Says she's concentrating on graduating—just summer school and work— and doesn't want to be distracted." I took a long drink of beer and stared down at the lake feeling eighteen, my mind snugly blank.

"Yeah, we'll see how long that'll last. I give it till Fourth of July. So does this mean she's given up on you?"

"Shit, she gave up a long time ago. Things are pretty okay between us now. I don't see too much of her since I moved downtown, close to campus but not close enough to be convenient for her."

"I guess that's good. I mean, I know it was a bitch, her always acting like your girlfriend at parties and stuff. You took it pretty well though, I have to say." Michael gulped his beer and opened another, pointing to the can: "Can't let 'em get warm."

"Nope."

The sun dropped quickly behind the clouds, the pink-orange dimming into lavender, shadows fading around us.

"David, I want to tell you something."

"Okay."

"I need to tell you this but I don't want to weird you out or anything and please don't tell Lexy yet because I want to talk to her too and it's really no big deal but it is and it's important that I talk to you and . . . ."

"Hey, slow down, bud. We're not in a hurry, are we?" It always made me nervous when people told me they were going to tell me something. It would've always been much easier if they just went ahead and told me. And it was never anything good either. Besides, I sensed what Michael was going to say. The sun slipped beneath the hills and I became suddenly chilled. I reached for another beer. "What is it, buddy? Just tell me."

He took a long drink from the can of beer. "It's just that, well, it's just that I'm gay, that's all. No big deal."

I continued looking at the disappearing sun, blinking my eyes to focus. And all I could think about was how Michael was my best friend ever, how he knew almost everything about me and that it was all okay with him. I wanted to tell him that his news didn't affect me but felt paralyzed by my own fear.

And then I thought about when we lived in the frat house during college. I had been dating a Deke little sister at the time and Michael had been going out with this Chi O from his art class. One night late, after I got back from the library, I knocked on Michael's door and went in. He was getting stoned, listening to the Talking Heads, making sketches of his foot, which was propped on an open dresser drawer. He held out the bong to me, "Want some?"

I lit up and sat on the floor, and we started talking about the usual stuff—school, music, people we knew. He set his sketch pad on the dresser and pulled out a couple Penthouses from the drawer. He tossed one at me, and we started reading the letters out loud, dramatically, laughing as we began: "I never in a *million* years thought *I'd* ever have an experience to write to Penthouse magazine about, *but . . . .*"

Michael said the letters turned him on even more than the pictures, and after about a half hour of reading and toking Michael said the pot was making him really horny and asked if it was okay with me if he jerked off. He said I should too, no big deal. I knew I shouldn't have, but I did. And it was more fun being with a guy—sort of, even though we hardly touched each other—than I wanted it to be. We never talked about it, or did it again, though secretly I really wanted to. I was scared; clueless about what it could mean, about what being gay was all about.

45

"Say something, David. Anything is okay. I just want to be your friend. Nothing's changed, okay?"

"Are you sure you are . . . ."

"Gay? It's all right to say it, really. Yes, I'm sure. Look, this just makes life more interesting, right?" Michael tried to laugh. "We don't have to talk about it if you don't want to."

"No, it's okay, really. I'm glad you told me. So you're gay, what do you want me to say?"

"Well . . . ." Michael let out a breath. "You could say, 'that's great, Michael, I'm so glad you're gay. I'm so lucky to have my first gay friend. Gay is good. It's a good thing, Michael. Very, very good. Now you and Lexy can go out cruising for guys together.'"

We started laughing and every time we began to stop Michael said something else that made us laugh. On our third beer, Michael said, "And I'm thinking about moving to Houston."

"Houston? You're not even finished with school yet." I felt sick, like I was going to throw up.

"Yeah, I think I am. I need a break. It's been a bitch of a year for me, dealing with this and . . . ."

"What the hell are you going to do in Houston?"

"Get a job. And just be gay, I guess. Got any ideas?"

I didn't, and the following Friday Michael called me at work and said he was leaving the next day. He told me to go ahead and tell Lexy everything for him because he didn't think he could deal with her after all.

That evening I went straight home after work and Lexy was there. She had convinced my landlady to let her in and had cooked this fancy Italian dinner.

I tossed my jacket over a chair and loosened my tie. "What's the deal, Lex?" I took a glass of wine from her, kissed her cheek and followed her into the kitchen.

"Surprise," she spoke quietly, and opened the oven to parmesan starting to brown over manicotti. The smell of basil and garlic spilled into the room.

"Geez, Lex, this is great, why'd you do all this?" I took a sip of the Chianti and picked a black olive out of the salad bowl sitting on a wet cutting board.

"I just wanted a good dinner in." She turned to me and picked up her glass. "With a good friend." She lifted the glass in front of her face.

I finished my wine on the toast and refilled my glass and topped off Lexy's. We chatted in the kitchen as Lexy dressed the salad and sprinkled shelled sunflower seeds across its top.

"What's wrong, David? You seem weird."

"It's been a long week. I'm just in a quiet mood. *You* can talk though."

"No, that's okay. Quiet is good sometimes. We can have a quiet evening."

"I'm really glad you did all this though." I didn't want to cry. "Everything smells great."

During dinner we drank a second bottle of wine, finishing it later in the living room. I put on a Neil Young CD and sat near Lexy on the couch, staring into the candle on the coffee table, the only light in the room. During "Heart of Gold" I turned to Lexy and covered her hand with mine. She stared into my eyes and I didn't turn away.

I felt suddenly so alone, just as my life was supposed to be beginning again. I knew nothing could stop the changes, but I couldn't help feeling like a block of ice that had been tossed into a pool of water, invisible currents directing its movement as it slowly became smaller and smaller before finally disappearing altogether. But Lexy was there, warm by my side, our bodies coming together on the couch, and all I remember is this incredibly safe feeling, an intense muscular tiredness washing over my body, making me close my eyes and want to sleep forever.

4

"It's far from finished, but I really love this piece."
Michael scratched at the light stubble on his chin as he spoke
of his new sculpture's progress. "My heart was really into it,
you know—and then she pulled out just because her husband
is a bigot. He didn't want her working with a queer. And of
course she has no balls."

"Of course." I had already heard the story twice.

Michael and I were driving to Aunt Ivy's farm. I'd taken
off the top to my Jeep before we left Austin because I liked the
feel of the rushing wind, especially once we were out of town.

"I know I shouldn't have accepted the commission, but
man, I could've lived off that other ten thousand for the rest of
the year. The whole thing just gets to me. Now what am I
going to do?" He drummed his hands on his right thigh.

"Yeah, it sucks, but maybe it's for the best. You told me you didn't have control from the very beginning." The music on KLBJ started fading in and out as we drove south past its range, so I turned off the radio. "Just keep reminding yourself that she didn't back out because of the work itself. It was because she's spineless—and her husband is a prick."

"You're right." Michael turned away from me and looked out across a field near San Marcos, on which concrete had been poured for yet another outlet mall. A few high clouds drifted overhead.

"Well, *I'm* still excited about seeing the piece, mostly because of the sounds you've been talking about."

"Yeah, me too, I guess." Michael picked up the tempo of his thigh drumming. "Remember the other week at Laguna Gloria when we saw those humongous wind chime tubes? The longest one had to have been ten feet long and a foot around."

"Yeah, they were pretty incredible." I remembered the deep, hollow tones, blending together and resonating throughout the grounds, like something I'd imagine hearing at a Shinto monastery.

"I thought they were pretty haunting, but definitely beautiful. They had pathos, man, real pathos." Michael looked as though he had entered his own little reverie, his eyes slightly closed and his head bobbing, his hair tossed by the wind. "That's the type of effect I'm thinking about with Copper One. That's the work's tentative name, Copper One."

"Sounds like a space probe: 'Copper One calling Earth, come in Earth. Earth?'"

"It does, huh? Well, then you can help me come up with a new name. Anyway, the wind chime at Laguna Gloria had six tubes. I only want a five-tone scale, so I'm thinking the effect will be more Eastern or transcendental, I don't know, maybe even mournful. I'm still waiting for the exact inspiration."

"Can't wait to hear it." I was actually quite enthused about hearing it but wondered why I held back from letting Michael know.

"Well, you might be in for a long wait. I've got enough money, but I'm still sort of stuck right now—artistically." Several waves of low clouds had moved overhead and Michael took off his sunglasses and tossed them in the open glove box.

"That's okay, I'm a patient guy. Besides . . ."

"Yeah, I know, '. . . and besides, anticipation is half the fun.' Somehow this doesn't feel that fun to me."

There were no cars on the rural stretch of road after I turned off the highway. I slowed to forty-five on the narrow strip of patched asphalt bordered by ditches thick with bamboo like cane thickets. Beyond the ditches were fields of ripening corn. The stalks were withered and beginning to brown. Other fields lay recently plowed, their black soil graying in the heat of the day.

The passing air became earthy and dense. Unlike the limestone terrain west of Austin, there were no junipers, and only an occasional oak tree. The landscape's uncultivated highlands had become dense pastures of mesquite trees, scraggly brush and prickly pear cactus. Cedar elm and hackberry dominated the lower wooded pastures of the Santa Clara Creek valley.

I pulled in front of the farm's gate and handed Michael the key to the padlock. He hopped out of the Jeep and unlocked the chain that held the metal gate closed against the barbwire fence. The rusted words "O.T. Krueger Farm" were welded inside a rectangular frame screwed into a silvered cedar post. Michael jumped on the gate as it swung open. After I drove through he closed the gate and I heard the lock click closed.

We passed the tin-roofed wooden barn and wound into a back pasture, following the dry ruts cut into the compacted earth. At the top of a low hill I stopped the Jeep in the middle of the road, turned off the engine, and we got out.

"It's really dusty up here." Michael squinted and pulled a joint from his t-shirt pocket and a lighter from his jeans.

"It's the wind, and the sandier dirt. We'll be going that way." I pointed west into the dense brush that hid the valley.

"Things are much better down there." We started walking and I heard the scratch of the lighter.

We passed the joint as we walked, following a cattle trail through the mesquite brush and prickly pear, down toward the creek. The jackrabbits and cottontails had eaten most of the wild grasses, so the clearings were barren except for tufts of unappetizing weeds. We stopped occasionally to look down an armadillo hole or to examine pieces of flint rock, checking if any were parts of arrowheads, as Aunt Ivy had shown me.

By the time we reached the creek the earlier clouds were gone and the sky was completely clear. Yellowish brown sandstone rocks, some the size of cars, lay along the shallow, flowing water. Michael and I jumped from rock to rock, crossing the narrow creek, back and forth, several times, as I led him to what Aunt Ivy had called Picnic Rock. It was a large, flat oval partly buried beneath earth and water next to a half-sphere one, which she called Turtle Rock. I set my backpack on Picnic Rock and took out a water bottle. I looked up at the sky and noticed the wind moving through the upper reaches of a native pecan tree. The tapered green leaves fluttered, exposing branches loaded with the tree's small, green-husked nuts.

Michael stood on top of Turtle Rock, arms outstretched, and pumped himself up and down on his toes. "This place is fucking fantastic. How come you never brought me out here before?"

"I guess I've always thought of it as a sort of a secret place. I've always come alone, except of course when I was a kid and Aunt Ivy and I would drive out here." I took off my shirt and lay on the warm rock, looking at my reflection and the sunlight shimmering on the surface of the clear water. "I hadn't been here for about a year until last week when I got the urge to come out."

Michael took off his shoes and socks and cuffed his jeans. "Man, I could live out here forever. The isolation is incredible." Using the smooth white stones that lay along the creek bed, he began to build a dam across a section of quick flowing water less than six inches deep. "You said this was near the middle of the property?"

"Yeah, about."

"And how big is it?"

"About eight hundred and fifty acres."

"That's pretty incredible, don't you think? That it's all yours now?"

"Yeah, I guess." I closed my eyes, content to be in one of my favorite places and alone with Michael.

"How'd your aunt come to have this place?"

"It wasn't always hers. Her older sister and brother-in-law lived out here until he died. That's when Aunt Clara moved to San Antonio." I rolled over onto my stomach, turning my head to watch Michael construct his dam.

"Were they close?"

"Who?"

"Your aunt and her sister?" Michael stood up straight and stretched his arms toward the sky.

"Maybe when they were kids, but not later. Aunt Ivy told me she thought Clara resented her for having had more opportunities when she was young."

"Like what?" Michael continued placing rocks as a foundation for his dam from bank to bank, a span of about five feet.

"Clara stayed on in their parent's farmhouse after she married Otto. He took over the farming from his father-in-law, and she took care of her mother and father . . . ."

"So what did Aunt Ivy get? You still haven't answered my question."

"I know, just a second." I turned on my side and propped my head on my hand. "It's like her parents were very tight, sort of like misers. They didn't spend much money on their kids because they were always worried about their future."

Michael stopped working on his little dam, still standing in the shallow creek, and looked at me with his hands on his hips. "So . . . ."

"So, well, they found the money to send Aunt Ivy to Europe sometime after 1920 to study music."

"That was pretty cool of them, huh?"

"*I* think so, but I don't think Aunt Clara thought it was so cool. Anyway, Aunt Ivy met my Uncle August in Germany. He was the principal violist for the Berlin Philharmonic. Her piano instructor, this older guy who also played in the orchestra's string section, introduced them."

"God, David. How do you know all this?"

The soothing heat of the sun and the warm rock against my body made me sleepy. "Aunt Ivy didn't have a TV, so she told me stories instead. It seems like there's nothing I don't know about her life."

Michael turned away and knelt to pick up a football-size rock near a patch of watercress at the creek's edge. He strategically placed it on a low spot along his dam. The upstream level had risen a couple of inches behind the line of piled rocks, forcing the water to tumble. I liked hearing the gurgling and seeing the water bubble beneath Michael's dam. He rested on the turtle rock, captivated by seeing his creation at work, his bare feet drying in the sun. He wiped his hands on his jeans before pulling off his shirt and lighting another joint.

I had never met any of Aunt Ivy's family besides Clara. Soon after she had moved to San Antonio, she became a part of my Sunday afternoons with Aunt Ivy. Getting to know a relative was a novelty, though she didn't live long enough for me to get to know her very well.

What quickly became a weekend ritual with Aunt Clara began a month after she settled into a retirement condominium in Olmos Park, another old-money neighborhood near Alamo Heights, when I was thirteen. She had been waiting outside of her building when Aunt Ivy and I came by to pick her up in the white Oldsmobile Eighty-Eight. Aunt Clara looked so different than Aunt Ivy. She was much heavier and somewhat shorter. She always wore her gray hair in a bun on top of her head, and she preferred loose cotton dresses, which made her look as if she never left her home.

We drove down Hildebrand Avenue to Broadway and Aunt Ivy parked in the small lot behind Earl Abel's. It was already one o'clock but Aunt Ivy said she liked the restaurant better after all the old people had left, which I thought was pretty funny.

"Hello, ladies. How are we doing today?" asked the beehive haired hostess of around sixty-five before turning her attention to me. "And you, young man?" We said fine, and she seated us at a table up against a large aquarium in the center of the main dining room. An oversized, zebra-striped angelfish swam to the glass and looked in my direction.

Both Aunt Ivy and Aunt Clara ordered the lunch special: poached cod with green beans and mashed potatoes, fresh cranberry salad on a lettuce leaf, and a cup of coffee. I had a hamburger, French fries and a Coke. As our waitress was about to leave our table, Aunt Clara called her back and ordered a whiskey sour for Aunt Ivy, and one for herself.

By the time our food was served, Ivy and Clara had already told more than a half-dozen stories about dead relatives. At the end of each anecdote, they toasted the guest ghost, making sure I lifted my Coke glass to a proper height.

". . . and Otto bottle-fed that black calf every day after its mama died, right up until it could manage on its own." Aunt Clara drank from her cocktail.

"He always took such good care of his animals." Aunt Ivy lowered her head and smoothed her white napkin, which lay folded on the table in front of her.

Aunt Clara drained her drink and wiped the corner of her mouth with a finger. She picked out the maraschino cherry from the bottom of the small glass and held it, absentmindedly dangling it by its stem with her elbow propped on the table. "Go ahead, Ivy, tell David about Otto, about how you used to be sweet on him when he and I first started going around together."

"Oh Clara, for heaven's sake, I was a girl. I merely thought he was a very kind and gentle man. He reminded me of Daddy."

"Ivy, dear, I still like to tease you after all these years." Aunt Clara laughed, showing her large yellowed teeth, as our waitress arrived and began positioning plates in front of us.

The angelfish swam behind tendrils of bottlebrush growing from a thick layer of beige aquarium gravel. Aunt Clara sipped from her coffee, looked up at the waitress, and opened her fingers so that the bright red cherry dropped into the center of her lightly peppered potatoes.

After a while my marijuana daze cleared and I felt restless. I sat up and pulled on my shirt. "I want to show you a little more of the farm before we leave, okay?"

"Great. You can bring me here anytime. I'm serious, I love this place." Michael put on his socks and shirt, and we sat near each other on Picnic Rock as we tied our sneakers.

We continued hiking up through the elm woods on the other side of the creek and toward the Coastal Bermuda grass field. We passed by a few cows, black Angus, on their way to the creek for water. It was the same breed Aunt Ivy told me her father had always kept.

I had extended the cattle lease she had granted to the rancher who owned the adjacent place. He had run cattle on the farm ever since Uncle Otto died. I enjoyed having cows around, watching them eat and hearing them bellow. I looked forward to seeing the newborn calves the following spring. Aunt Ivy had told me she loved visiting Clara and Otto each spring because of the new calf crop.

Michael and I continued walking along the dirt road toward a jerry-built barbwire and cedar post gate. It kept the cows off the field until the grass could rebound from a prior feeding. I ungapped the fence and laid it open, and we walked through to the forty acre field.

Michael stood on the crest of a terrace created years before to direct rainwater through the field. "There's nothing out here, except a lot of trampled grass."

"There's a huge pond over there, a stock tank. You can barely see it from here." I pointed to a distant circle of reflection.

"Yeah, I see it. What's that sticking out of it?"

"It's a dock. They used the pond as a swimming hole. It's where Aunt Ivy's son Karl drowned."

"Really?" Michael's began to walk faster. Soon we were near the only large tree at the center of the field, an old gnarled mesquite a few yards from the edge of the pond. Its trunk was thick, and both living and dead limbs spread low. Mesquite brush and small willows also grew near the pond. Several boards were missing from a gray pinewood dock that extended from the dry grass. It lay over a wide ring of mud and out ten more feet, ending over the water. Stands of cattails grew at the water's edge, and cow tracks were punched deep into the mud. Michael followed as I slowly tested the dock and then walked out to its end. We sat on the edge, dangling our feet above the surface of the murky water. It was hard for me to believe that someone had drowned in such a simple body of water.

I had lived with Aunt Ivy for almost two years before she took me to the farm. One evening in early April after dinner, as we sat on the couch talking, she dropped her slender hands into her lap and said, "David, I think we should take a drive out to the farm tomorrow. You know, with Clara gone, it's all ours now."

"Sure, that sounds great, what time do you want—"

"I haven't been out there in years and the weather's been so pleasant. What with all the winter rain, the wildflowers must be beautiful. I don't remember if I ever told you, but your cousin Karl is buried there."

"Really? Where at?"

"In a small, hidden meadow that my father left especially to me in his will. Of course, it is a sad place, but it's not really sad, David." She wiped near her eyes with the back of her hand. "We'll go there tomorrow. I'll write a note for your school saying that you're ill."

The next day we drove for more than an hour and ended up fifty miles south of the city along the Santa Clara Creek. Aunt Ivy's parents had named Aunt Clara after it. Aunt Ivy had told me she liked visiting the farm right before Easter because there was so much promise in the air with everything newly green.

The Olds took the final dirt road like a truck and we parked by a fence where a narrower path began. I grabbed the picnic basket and the jar of iced lemonade from the back seat and Aunt Ivy tied on her straw hat with its yellow ribbon and brought along a pair of kitchen scissors.

I followed her down to the creek. After we spread the blue-and-white checked cloth across the picnic rock, Aunt Ivy pointed to Turtle Rock and told me she used to sit on it as a young girl, straddling its shell as she pretended to ride "through the South Pacific searching for sunken pirate ships full of gold and silver treasures."

The creek was clear enough to see the sun perch and baby bass that darted beneath the lily pads, moving in and out of the rounds of shade. Farther down from us the water spilled over a fallen log and into a shallow pool before becoming slow and deep in the distance.

"It's just like you told me it was." I pointed at the creek flowing around us. "I love watching the fish and hearing the water. Hey Aunt Ivy, you think when I get my driver's license, I can come out here sometimes?"

"Of course you may, David, as long as you promise to bring me along once in a while."

"Deal."

Aunt Ivy set out paper plates and napkins and a jar of her sliced, sweet bread-and-butter pickles. She unwrapped the smoked turkey sandwiches we had picked up at the deli on Broadway. She lifted a translucent blue Tupperware bowl out of the basket. "Now, these are for later." She smiled at me, raising an eyebrow.

"What kind are they, oatmeal?"

"No, they're chocolate chip." She smiled again.

"All right, Aunt Ivy!"

After taking one bite from her sandwich, she set it down and sipped from her lemonade. "David, I think you're quite old enough to hear the story about what happened to Karl."

"You said he drowned when he was a baby, right?" I stopped eating.

"Yes, it was at the pond, here on the farm. It was so very long ago and I try not to think about it too often anymore, but I believe it's something you should know."

"You can tell me, if you want." I looked away from her eyes.

She ran her hands across the cloth napkin that lay on her lap. "For Karl's first birthday, August and I had planned to have a picnic here on the farm near the pond. It was the spring of 1924." She smiled. "The wildflowers were at their peak early that April. Oh David, they were marvelous. I hope they're as beautiful for you today."

"When are we going to see them?" I began eating again.

"Soon, after we're through with our lunch." She covered her sandwich with her napkin and continued. "Our picnic was under a young mesquite tree, which was just beginning to leaf out near the edge of the pond. I was helping Clara unwrap sausages, cheeses and breads and such on the heavy quilt she had spread out to protect against fallen mesquite thorns.

"August was playing with Karl on the dock, dipping his feet into the water. That darling boy was laughing and kicking at its surface. Oh David, he was such a joyful little thing." Aunt Ivy closed her eyes and placed a crooked finger in front of her mouth. She remained that way for a moment, steeling herself. "And then Otto joined August on the dock with two more bottles of beer.

"August yelled to me that Karl needed to begin learning how to swim that very day."

"Why? He was just a baby." I had finished my sandwich and was starting to think about the chocolate chip cookies.

"I know, David. Sometimes I think that man must have been crazy." Her voice lowered to a whisper. "He said he had read a journal article that said swimming had been proven instinctual for humans, as it was for dogs."

"Is that true?"

"I didn't care if it was, so of course I told him no. It was too cool for even me to be in my bathing suit. He argued with me but finally agreed to wait until Karl was older. I so regret having left them, but August had promised, and Otto was there . . . ." She started to cry, almost imperceptibly. I drew in my legs and held them with my arms as I listened.

She wiped the tears from her face and looked down at the water flowing around the picnic rock and then cleared her throat. "Clara and I had walked a short distance behind a terrace and were picking bluebonnets. When I stood up and turned toward the pond I saw August pick him up. My baby boy was giggling and I was happy he was in such good spirits on his special day. August swung him back and forth. From behind the terrace, I didn't realize they were still on the dock.

"And then, oh David, when I heard that splash, Clara and I ran toward the pond as quickly as we could." Aunt Ivy dropped her face into her hands and shook it for a moment before looking back up toward me, her eyes filling with tears. "Then we heard a louder splash, and when we made it to the dock, Otto was white as a sheet and said August had gone in after Karl . . . ."

"Why did Uncle August throw him in?" I poured more lemonade.

"I'll never understand it." Her tears had stopped and her face looked as if it was cast in concrete.

"When Clara and I reached the end of the dock we were screaming. Oh David, it was the most horrible moment of my life. I was in full panic and jumped into the pond where Otto had pointed. I was wearing those awful old lace-up shoes and a long skirt and wouldn't have made it back to the dock if Otto hadn't kicked off his shoes and jumped in after me. I remember so vividly Clara screaming on the dock as Otto pulled me out of the water.

"When August finally appeared at the surface, he said he couldn't find Karl, and went under again. I remember feeling that I couldn't breathe and thought I would die. I actually thought I was going to die."

"Oh my God, Aunt Ivy, I can't believe you went through all that and can even talk about it." I reached out and held her soft, eighty-year-old hands.

"Clara later said I went into shock at that point. I don't remember anything after that, until we buried him the next day. Otto had stayed up into the night to build the little coffin." She turned away from me and looked up at the sky as a flurry of sparrows moved from one elm to another.

"I don't how I was able to leave the pond with Clara or how I ever stopped crying, or why I never got to see him." She again wiped at her cheeks. "That was all so long ago, David. It's hard to imagine, but I remember much of it all so clearly."

I felt sick, sort of floating and hollow, after listening to her. But trying to understand that she was really there, that it wasn't just a story, made me feel even worse. I tried to imagine what Karl must have felt, having so much fun one minute and so cut off from the world the next, waiting for his dad to save him. It hurt too much to even try. I just sat next to Aunt Ivy on the safe warmth of our picnic rock, staring into the creek. I could see straight through to the bottom and yet still see my blank face rippling on the water's slow flowing surface.

Aunt Ivy leaned toward me and patted me on the back. "Neither of us feels very good right now, I know, but it's okay to be sad sometimes." She sighed deeply, stared off into the woods, and then picked up her napkin and dabbed at the perspiration that had formed on her brow.

We finished our picnic in silence, though Aunt Ivy barely touched her food. After gathering our things, we walked up out of the creek valley and through the woods a short distance to the meadow where Karl was buried, adjacent to the Coastal Bermuda field that cradled the stock pond.

We walked out toward the middle of the more gently terraced field, which was thick with color and scent. Our pace was slowed by the thick tangle of wildflowers, which were oblivious to our presence or the passage of time, seemingly content to stage their show for only butterflies and bees. A tingling sensation worked its way up from the base of my spine as Aunt Ivy placed a hand on my shoulder and squeezed.

The entire meadow spilled away from us, blanketed with endless mounds of soft, fragrant bluebonnets, their lupine blossoms interspersed with random sprays of reddish pink Indian paintbrush, yellow buttercups and lavender phlox. The sunny afternoon's gentle breeze gave the hidden meadow a billowy, surrealistic hum. I felt flushed, feverish even, as soft waves of electrical energy lapped at something inside me and then subsided, as though they had succeeded in nudging my soul loose from my body. It was as if I could see myself standing there, but it was clearly not all of me. I stood very still, trying to remain aware of every sensation. I'd never felt so free from my world, feeling lightheaded as I dropped to my knees and sank into the airy cushion of the wildflowers. The warmth from the earth seemed to support me as I rose above the field, where everything appeared more focused and even more beautiful than from below. And then I saw my body just sitting there, collapsed looking, as if waiting for me to return. It was then, in that floating space, that I heard the wildflowers whisper to me: "Come back down to us. We have plans for you. Come back."

I no longer spoke when I was able to stand up, and then continued following Aunt Ivy through the meadow, trembling.

"Are you feeling all right, David?" Her voice was barely audible.

I tried to tell her about my experience and she smiled, nodding, again touching my shoulder. "You're lucky, it doesn't always happen. But you must never talk about it—if you want it to ever happen again." She held a finger in front of her lips and shook her head. "I don't know why. It's what Daddy told me and it's true." I didn't protest, nor did I even want to know more. For the first time in my life, belief was enough.

We picked as many flowers as we could hold and arranged a nest of them on Karl's grave in front of a small cement cross, its edges worn smooth by decades of wind and weather. For the Easter bunny to put his eggs in, Aunt Ivy explained, as if I were five instead of fourteen. She removed her hat and knelt at the grave with her hands together on her lap. I stood behind, watching the sun flicker through her grayish white hair, spackling the cross with its light.

We walked the mile back to the car and drove home, a bouquet of wildflowers for the piano vase lying in the back seat. Just as she pulled the car into her garage she broke the drive's silence. "He was a very good boy, you know, very well behaved. Just an angel." She almost laughed. "He'd be over fifty now. Can you imagine, Little Karl, middle-aged?"

"That's where Karl is buried." I pointed toward the meadow, spent and drying into stems and seeds. Michael and I were walking back to the Jeep.

"You want to stop off at the grave?"

"No, we've been here too long already." I couldn't see the cross through the tall Johnson grass along the fence line. "But I could go for a beer. Are you in a hurry to get back to Austin?"

"Me, in a hurry? Yeah, I got a cake in the oven. Let's get a move on, buddy." Michael laughed and slapped my shoulder as he jogged past me.

After locking the gate's padlock, I drove about five miles and pulled up in front of what looked like an abandoned shack with a faded green sign reading "Mueller's General Store." The building leaned to the left, its gray clapboard siding flecked with white paint. An old Chevy pickup was parked out front, next to a leafy chinaberry tree that seemed to support the tired old building.

I pushed the metal "Drink Coca-Cola" handle on the ripped screen door and we walked inside. Light from four open windows faintly illuminated narrow floor-to-ceiling shelves along the left side of the store, showing canned goods, rat traps and dog food. Brooms and mops hung from hooks between the windows. The right side of the room was partitioned by a long wooden bar. Tilted, open boxes of nuts, bolts and washers lined the wall behind the bar, which ended at a refrigerated meat-and-cheese display case near the front of the store. A black cat lay curled on a white-enameled scale on top of the display case. The scale's needle, which moved delicately with the cat's breathing, hovered around sixteen pounds.

Michael and I were looking at seed packages on a circular wire rack when the proprietor I'd seen the week before stepped through a darkened doorway behind the bar. He combed his white hair to the side with his fingers and smacked his lips. He looked at least eighty years old.

"Can I help you boys?" The old man spoke in our direction. The cat lifted its head to look at us and then lowered it again. Michael and I walked to the bar.

"Couple of Millers?" I looked at Michael and he nodded.

The man turned to Michael. "High Life okay?"

Michael almost laughed and I said, "That'd be fine, thanks."

The storekeeper opened the beer box lid and lifted out three clear bottles. He opened them behind the bar and I heard the caps clink into a tin can on the floor. He set two bottles on the bar and took a sip from the third.

"So, what's the good word, gentlemen?" He shooed the cat off the scale, as if it were the first time he'd seen it there. Before I could answer, he looked directly at me. "Say, you were in here last week, weren't you?"

I told him yes, surprised he remembered. "You had a few more customers that day."

"There's hardly anyone here most times, what with everyone driving to town for everything these days, except for the old folks. Well, that's the way things go in this world, I guess." He sighed and then smiled, extending his right hand across the bar. "It's nice to see you again. Mueller, Henry Mueller. And you are?" He cupped his hand around a red-tinted ear, enlarged and softened with age.

"David Thorpe," I shook his hand, "and this is my friend Michael. We're from Austin."

"Austin, huh? I haven't been up there in those parts since I was a boy. "I'm lucky if I make it to Seguin a couple times a year, and that's only fifteen miles away." He laughed and poured beer into a small frosted glass. "So what brings you down here."

"I inherited some land up the road along the Santa Clara, the O.T. Krueger farm." Michael had wandered to the front of the store.

"Oh yes." He sounded excited. "I know it well, very well for sure. Old man Krueger used to let me hunt rabbits there when I was a youngster. That's one beautiful piece of land." He smiled and drank from his glass, leaving a foam mustache above his lip. "So what's your relation?"

"Did you know Clara and Otto?" I began working the soggy label off my beer bottle with a fingernail.

"I sure did. Otto used to buy feed from the store. He sure was a decent fellow and a right good farmer." He emptied the remainder of his beer into his glass. "He always made a crop."

"Well, Clara and her younger sister Ivy were sisters of my great grandfather, who died as a young man . . . ."

"Which is why Clara ended up with the farm. Yes, I remember. I heard Clara died a while back, after she moved to the city."

"That's right, and, then her sister, my Aunt Ivy, got the farm. She died almost three months ago." I drank from my beer bottle, proud that I could communicate the connection. "And because there's no other family, I ended up with the farm."

Michael joined us and set his empty beer bottle on the bar. "Excuse me, do you have a bathroom?"

"Through there." Mr. Mueller pointed at the back door, which stood half open and hung by one hinge. "Follow the trail about twenty yards and you'll see the outhouse."

"Thanks." Michael turned away from Mr. Mueller and brushed up against me, whispering, "This place is a kick. We've *got* to come back." I nodded, smiling, and Michael walked out through the doorway.

"You're pretty lucky to have all that land at your age. What are you going to do with it?"

"I don't have any plans."

"You could get a pretty penny for it, what with all the folks moving out to the country from San Antonio, building all those big fancy houses."

"I'd never sell it, that much I know."

"You say that now, but money has a way of changing that sentiment."

I looked around and saw Michael through the screen door, walking toward the store. He joined us again at the bar.

Mr. Mueller nodded to Michael and then turned toward me. "So you knew Ivy Krueger? Now she was a looker."

"Well, Ivy Schumann. Yes, she was my great-great aunt."

"Oh that's right, Schumann. She married that fellow from Germany. Quiet man, not very friendly. What was his name?" Mr. Mueller tilted his head back, closing his eyes.

"August."

"Oh yes, August. I only met the man a couple times when they came out to visit Clara. Otto would bring him here for a few beers. Too bad about that baby of theirs, horrible accident." Mr. Mueller shook his head as he grabbed three more beers from the cooler. After opening them, he slid two toward Michael and me.

"Yeah, I was pretty shocked when I first heard about it." I took a sip from my beer. Michael sat on the bar and held his bottle between his legs. He began petting the cat, which was back on the scale.

"Hard to believe they never found that baby's body." Mr. Mueller filled his glass too quickly and beer foam slid down its side.

"What?" I set my bottle on the bar. "What do you mean, they never found the body? The grave is on the farm, I've seen it."

"Well, yes. There is a grave, but there's nobody buried there. I'm sorry, I guess there's no way you could have known that." Mr. Mueller drank from his glass, his hand shaking, spilling beer onto the bar.

"What are you saying? How do you know this?" I looked into Mr. Mueller's eyes and then down at the bar, which was smeared wet with bottle rings.

"I was just a kid helping my dad here at the store after school, you see. I was taking a pop break one afternoon when Otto was the only customer in the store drinking beer with my father. Well, he started telling Dad about that drowning. He said he and August did their best to find that boy, but that their drag line never caught, despite running it over and over."

"Why didn't they call someone to help?" The shadows became less distinct in the store as the outside light faded.

"I figure they thought it was too late. It's never made much sense to me either." Mr. Mueller sat on a low stool behind the bar.

"August convinced Otto not to tell Ivy and Clara that they couldn't find the boy. He told the women that it would be better if he and Otto handled the body before the burial, so as to spare Ivy any more grief."

"They *never* found the body?" I looked at Mr. Mueller and then at Michael, who was staring at me.

"That's what Otto said. He made us swear never to tell, for Ivy's sake, and said that Clara could never know either. Dad never said anything. Hell, I figure everyone's dead now, and well, you're their kin, so you got a right to know. There's nothing anyone can do about it now."

Mr. Mueller refused our money for the second round, and Michael and I walked out the front door into the darkening glow of a long completed sunset.

"Give me the keys, I'll drive." Michael held out his hand.

I did as he said, walked around to the other side of the Jeep, and glanced up at the cloud streaked horizon, which looked as if iron filings had been spilled across the blue gray sky.

5

The pink glow of a halogen streetlight cast a moving shadow in front of the Jeep as Michael pulled into my driveway and parked alongside his bicycle. I was tired from the day at the farm, tired in a way that made my head throb and reel, yet not tired enough to be able to sleep. Michael and I had barely spoken during the hour drive back to Austin. I sensed that he felt it better to delay any conversation he might be interested in pursuing, something that he was not very good at. "You want me to come in for a while?" he asked finally as he turned off the engine and placed the keys into my hand.

"Sure, if you want." I glanced at the shadowy bulk of my house, noticing how cold and rejected it looked at night. I looked down at the ring of keys in my hand. "I mean, I'd like for you to stay."

We got out of the Jeep and walked along the sidewalk to the front door. I wished I had turned on the porch light before I had left. I heard Abby's metal tags jingle on her collar as I unlocked the door. She jumped up on Michael and he petted her while I walked to the kitchen to get a glass of water.

"You got anything to drink?" Michael called from the living room where I could see him pulling at the knotted rope toy Abby clenched between her teeth. Her stifled growls always sounded more playful than menacing. She loved Michael, all the attention he gave her, his roughhousing, the weight of his touch.

"I think so, let me see." I opened the refrigerator and grabbed a Budweiser for Michael. He'd turned on the TV and was lounging on the couch. Abby lay on the rug in front of him, chewing her toy. I handed him the beer and settled into the overstuffed chair next to the couch. "You want to call for a pizza or something?"

"Nah, I'm not really hungry. Maybe later on. You?" Michael yawned and then drank from his beer.

"No, me neither." I finished my water.

Michael muted the TV with the remote control and turned his head toward me. "So, are you really okay with all the stuff that old man told you?"

"I guess there's not really anything to not to be okay about. It doesn't make me feel very good knowing that Uncle August lied to Aunt Ivy, but I guess I can understand why he did it." I glanced down at my lap. "He didn't want to make a bad situation worse." I was lying to Michael, trying to appear strong. Karl's death had devastated Aunt Ivy. I grabbed a square pillow from the floor and turned it over and over on my lap before stuffing it behind my head and slouching deeper into the chair.

"I can buy that, but don't you wonder why they didn't go for help? They could've just as easily told the truth and driven into town the next day and . . . ."

"I know, but . . . ."

"I bet ol' Otto never wanted to swim in *that* pond again." Michael lifted his shirt halfway up and began scratching his lower abdomen. "Wouldn't that be creepy, knowing that a decomposing baby . . . ."

I looked at Michael sharply and he stopped talking. Abby jumped on the large ottoman in front of my chair and walked in tight circles before curling her body into a ring at my feet.

Michael got up and went to the bookshelves across from the couch. He picked up a plastic replica of the Apollo 11 space capsule with a GI Joe outfitted in astronaut gear strapped inside, upside down.

"Where'd you get this?" He twirled the gray, blunt-nosed cone so that the sliding Plexiglas door faced me.

"It was in my old room at Aunt Ivy's house. I brought it here after she died."

Michael peered inside at the cardboard control panel upon which GI Joe's eyes were fixed. "Did you know 'ol Joe's missing a hand here?" Michael looked back at me. "Did Aunt Ivy buy this for you?"

"No, it's from my dad. He gave it to me in 1969, right after the moon-landing that summer." I remembered having enjoyed staging splashdowns in the bathtub with it, rescuing GI Joe from the dull gray ocean swells of my bath water, and then stripping off his chrome colored space outfit so we could bathe together before going to the Astronaut's Ball in Honolulu.

Michael looked at the patent-pending information stamped into the top near the GI Joe logo. "Good ol' Hasbro, merchandising history to the youth of America. It is pretty neat, though." He gripped the base of the foot-long capsule in front of him with an outstretched palm, squinting at it as if he were eyeing one of his works-in-progress. "I like the form. It's sort of phallic, don't you think?"

I laughed and stretched my arms back above my head, yawning. "Yeah, it is, huh?"

He began to slide open the Plexiglas door.

"No, don't, please." I jumped up and took the capsule from him. "It's really old and the door sort of sticks. Do you mind?"

"Sorry."

I returned it to the shelf and Michael lay back down on the couch, unmuted the TV and began flipping through the channels.

"No big deal." I clenched my hands into fists repeatedly and looked around the room.

Michael raised the volume on a baseball game, and we watched the Astros and the Cubs play, and he sipped at his beer.

By the fourth inning he had fallen asleep. The clock next to the space capsule read a quarter past nine. I picked up the remote, lowered and then muted the volume before turning off the lamp next to the couch. I leaned back and watched Michael sleep by the light of the TV. He had turned on his side and scrunched his legs forward, nesting into the couch as if he were cold. I went to get a blanket out of the hall closet and covered him with it. He mumbled, "Thanks, g'night," and sighed, and I settled back into my chair.

Michael looked like a little boy breathing through his mouth into a restful sleep, a sleep which I imagined would melt into playful dreams filled with joy and beautiful men with cocks the size of space capsules. I thought how adorable he appeared lying there, his blond, beard stubbled face nuzzled into the navy blue pillow, and the beige, fleece blanket tucked beneath his body. I wanted to touch his face and stroke his hair. I fantasized about sleeping alongside of him, feeling his body next to mine, matching my breath with his.

After a half hour of watching him sleep, fantasizing about the possibilities of a life of love with Michael, I walked over to him, kissed him lightly on the cheek, and returned to my chair. I began to pet Abby and then let out a deep breath and closed my eyes, giving into the sleep that had permeated the dimly lit room.

A blue sky lined with thin, orange-tinted clouds and filled with the sounds of chirping birds makes me smile as I hold out my arms and walk tightrope-fashion along a curb near a house in the Cedar Glen subdivision of San Antonio. The curb starts to move, tilting like a seesaw, and I begin to teeter when I notice the pink, strawberry ice cream stain on my green sweatshirt sleeve.

The clouds blow away in red wispy streams, leaving a darkening blue sky. In my new, white Keds I run along the sidewalk, which has the spring like feel of a trampoline, toward Sycamore Park, wishing for a skateboard like those owned by the older boys.

I shuffle through dried, hand-size leaves beneath the sycamore trees before running to the center of the park toward the playground, which pulses with patterns of greens and purples. I place one foot on the merry-go-round, hold on to the metal rail supports, and then push with my other foot into the shallow sand trench to build up speed. After several turns I close my eyes and lift my pushing foot onto the spinning disk and hold on tightly to the railing as the increasing force tries to throw me off. I enjoy the heart-quickening dizziness and the starbursts shooting beneath my eyelids, and then I begin to giggle, pretending I'm hurtling through space, out of control in a far-flung orbit. I open my eyes to a whirling blur of trees and houses. I don't understand how I will get off the merry-go-round as it spins faster and faster, and then I feel my fingers uncurl from the handles slowly, one at a time, and I lose my grip. I fly off and land hard in the sand trench. For a moment I cannot catch my breath. I wipe at the sand that has become imbedded in my cheek and see the grainy blood smear on my hand.

I hear laughing and turn to see my dad step from behind a large red-blooming oleander bush. I rub the remainder of the sand from my face and smile, before I get up and walk over to him.

"Had a bad fall, huh little man? C'mon, let's go home. Your mom'll patch you up. She always does, right?" He reaches out a huge, calloused hand and holds mine as we begin to walk toward our house.

It begins to rain, soft at first and then harder. I flinch and squeeze Dad's hand as I hear the first rumble of thunder. The drops grow larger and soon the ground isn't able to absorb them any longer. We splash in lockstep through ankle-deep water. The water is up to my knees by the time I see our house in the distance, obscured by the downpour. Mom is standing on the porch, waving her arm at us. But the more we walk, the farther away Mom and our house appear. The rain keeps falling, and the water becomes deeper and it becomes even more difficult to walk. Dad trudges ahead, my hand in his, guiding me through the deepening water. When the level approaches my shoulders, he lifts his arm so that our hands are free from the constraint of the flood. I look up and see the ice-cream stain darken and spread over my entire arm. I tilt my head even higher toward our clasped hands and the lightning streaked charcoal sky, and then I see my father slowly open his hand, just as the water begins to cover my head.

I woke, warm from agitated sleep and remembered my dream. The TV screen was silent snow and the clock on my bookshelf read a quarter of midnight. Michael was still asleep on the couch, the blanket bunched at his waist. Abby lifted her head, jumped off the ottoman, stretching her back legs behind her, and went into the kitchen. I heard her lap from her water bowl.

I stood up and went to the bookshelves and took down the space capsule, easily slid open its door and dislodged GI Joe from his fitted position, his left wrist merely a white plastic screw. I pulled out the envelope I had hidden in the cavity above the control panel more than fifteen years before.

The letter from my father had made me cry when I first received it. I had later agreed with Aunt Ivy that it would be best for me not to write him back, that I needed to let go of the past so I could move on with my life, but part of me had wanted to hold on to him. I stashed the letter above GI Joe and never wrote him back, and I never received another from him again. I told Aunt Ivy I'd thrown the letter away because she didn't want me to have any connection with him. "Don't forget what he did," she said, hugging me and patting my back. It didn't occur to me that she was referring to the murder.

· I sat near the light of the TV at the end of the couch and removed the sheet of notebook paper from the envelope. The last paragraph read: "I'm so sorry for putting you through all this, David. I know how hard things have been since your Mama died. Someday, when you're older and better able to understand, I hope to see you and have a chance to explain.

Regardless, I'm doing my time for it all, I guess. You're a good kid. I know your Aunt Ivy will take good care of you and give you everything you want. I'll write again. Love, Dad."

Michael rolled onto his side and mumbled. I turned off the silent TV, leaned against the couch and again listened to his breathing. I placed my hand on his forehead and stroked his hair several times before walking down the hall and into my room. I took off my clothes and climbed naked beneath the rumpled covers on my Craftmatic bed, which hadn't moved from its flat position in more than two months.

I lay on my back and stared at the gently moving shadow of the wisteria vine cast by a streetlight on my bedroom wall. I glanced toward the door when I heard light steps entering my bedroom, right before Abby jumped up on my bed and lay next to me in her usual spot.

6

A random pattern of mourning doves descended across the gray sky and dispersed as the birds banked their wings to soft landings on the grassy field next to the Jeep. I tucked my shirt and buttoned my jeans before walking to the barbwire fence alongside the stretch of rural highway. Michael continued peeing as another flock flew overhead, their wings whistling low in the distance. I could no longer see those that had landed, but I heard their hollow, sorrowful calls, amplified by the water standing in the marshy field.

Michael walked over to the fence just as the second grouping landed on the expansive field, which was scattered with reeds, cattails and tall grasses. "Cool birds, huh?"

"They're doves." I pulled a stem of Johnson grass out of a stalk near my leg and started to gnaw on the fleshy end with my back teeth, pretending to be the farm boy I'd always wanted to be.

"I've never seen any that weren't all white. You know, the kind in magic shows and at weddings."

"These are mourning doves, though some could be Mexican doves. I couldn't tell for sure, but it's not the season either way."

"The season?" Michael tugged at the grass stem in my mouth and smiled.

"Dove hunting season."

"How do you know when the season is?"

"I went hunting with my dad when I was a kid."

"Sounds real macho, David. Were they holding olive branches in their beaks as well?"

"I know it sounds psycho, but I never actually killed one. It was just fun being out in the country, trudging along the edges of pastures, absorbing nature in silence . . . ."

"With loaded guns." Michael raised his eyebrows.

"I know, I know. Come on, let's go. We still have another hour to drive."

We climbed into the Jeep and the view continued as before, flat land and billboards. Michael leaned his head against the side window and closed his eyes, and I drove the rest of the way to Huntsville, not believing I was making the trip.

I thought of the letter hidden in the space capsule and tried to remember my father. He seemed tall when I was a kid, but I don't remember if he actually was. His hair was black like mine and he kept it short, like a Marine's. He had always been at work by the time I woke up for school each morning and usually didn't get home until way after dark. When Mom died I was already old enough to stay home by myself, and so it seemed like I saw even less of him then. It was hard for me to imagine what she'd seen in him to make her want to marry him. They both had always been physically attractive, and maybe that was all that mattered when they first met because they were so young, but Dad definitely got the better end of the deal, except for the fact that Mom died and he got me. But Mom was always there for him, trim and well-groomed, ready to take care of all his needs and explain away his indiscretions. It made me mad that she never stood up to him. I figured it was because she was scared of him, too.

By the time I first went dove hunting with him, I had already begun to understand that I wasn't quite the son he'd hoped for. It had started the previous year when I was eight years old, my first and only summer in Little League. He had wanted, and expected, a pitcher or first baseman, but I was assigned an outfield position. He never went to any of the games. Mom made up excuses for him, like that he had important Saturday business meetings, excuses I wanted to believe.

He never really took his disappointment out on me, but Mom was a different story. One night when he thought I was asleep, after he'd had a few beers, I heard him lay into her in the kitchen, saying, "I can already tell, Vivian, David's going to grow up to be a faggot." I heard a glass break against the wall. "You couldn't even give birth to real son?" I squeezed a pillow over my head and thought about running circles in the backyard with Freckles until I was dizzy or climbing the highest tree in the world, so that no one could see me.

For the next few years I tried to come through for him, doing things I hated—anything to prove him wrong—things like playing baseball and football, and hunting for doves.

Dad and I woke up before dawn the morning of our first trip and drove about forty miles southeast of San Antonio to a ranch owned by his boss at the accounting firm. When we drove over the cattle guard at the gap in the electric fence, the clattering sound made me jump and look behind us. We continued to a spot at the edge of a freshly plowed field. I carried our paper sack lunches, which I had helped Mom prepare the night before, and Dad carried the guns. He had brought his twelve gauge shotgun, an automatic. For me, he had borrowed a four-ten, the lowest caliber there was, from a friend—from a woman, he pointed out.

He selected a spot, in the shade of the hackberry trees that lined the fence dividing a pasture from the field, and we crouched on the heavy, cloddy black earth and waited. We saw a few groupings of doves early on, too far away for a clear shot though, Dad said. After more than an hour of waiting for closer ones Dad said we could eat our lunch. I spread out the paper napkins Mom had enclosed and got out the ham and cheese sandwiches, potato chips, pickles wrapped in plastic, and cut-up apples covered with lemon juice to keep them from turning brown.

Dad pointed to the guns lying on the ground next to us and repeated his drill from the day before. "Shotguns are different from rifles, you see. Instead of a single bullet, these shells hold hundreds of small pellets, sort of like BBs." Dad held a couple of red, brass-capped shotgun shells in his hand, rattling them together as if they were dice. "See," he pointed to the crinkled end of one of the ribbed plastic shells. "When you fire, this explodes and the pellets eject and then spread in somewhat predictable patterns into the sky toward the doves. If you're lucky, enough pellets will hit one to bring it down." His grin faded as he turned his head toward me.

I looked at him, nodding, and took a bite of apple.

"The uses for shotguns are pretty limited, though, because you can't kill anything, besides birds, at much of a distance because of that scattering effect I just told you about." Dad gestured toward the sky with his hand. "But up close, shotguns are far more destructive than rifles."

When we finished eating, I began to pack up our stuff and Dad walked into the pasture a few yards. When he returned, he lit a cigarette, picked up his shotgun, and motioned with the barrel for me to follow.

We came across a small hackberry. Its trunk was about three inches in diameter. "David, I want to show you what I was talking about earlier." He held the gun at his waist, the barrel tip about two feet from the small tree trunk. "Cover your ears."

The blast spread out over the field, echoed back to us and was again pulled into the distance. The shot severed the tree, leaving a shredded blond wound about a foot long where the tree's top now bent to the ground. Frozen by the shock of the blast I didn't say a word, but only wondered why he had to kill the tree.

"Imagine what that could do to a man."

I could tell we were getting close to Huntsville because the "do not pick up hitchhikers" signs had begun along the highway. Michael woke from his nap, stretched and looked out the back window at the two flat strips of highway. He picked up a trampled magazine from the floorboard, looked at the cover, and then began to go through the stuff in my glove box.

"Do you really think you'll be able to see him today?"

"Why wouldn't they let me see him?"

"We *are* trying to visit a state prison. It's not like there's going to be a front desk clerk to ring your dad's suite and tell him to meet us in the lobby."

"What the hell else did you have to do today?" I looked toward him, angered by one of his rare moments of smug logic. A green road sign read "Huntsville 24."

"Nothing. I just wondered why you thought things would be so easy, that's all." Michael looked away from me and out his   window.

"Okay, so I'm a little freaked. I'm sorry. I know driving all this way on the spur of the moment is compulsive, but I wasn't thinking straight."

"You could've called."

"I know." I turned away from him and lowered my voice. "I could've done a lot of things."

Michael drank from the water bottle he had been holding between his legs and then offered it to me. I took a drink, pressed its top closed, and gave it back to him.

"I still can't believe your dad got twenty years for what might've been a hunting accident. That seems pretty severe."

"Yeah, I guess. I never really thought about it."

"Do *you* think it was an accident?"

"I guess I should, huh? Aunt Ivy thought he was guilty and thought I should too."

"Does it matter to you if the jury was right, that he meant to kill that guy?"

"I don't know, I guess not. Does that surprise you?"

"Everything you do lately surprises me." Michael leaned back in his seat, closed his eyes and lowered his voice. "What the hell, I'm just along for the ride."

I saw the main entrance behind a white brick guard post up the road, about a mile in front of the prison buildings. I slowed down and drove alongside a tall, thin guard who had stepped from the small building. He looked early middle-aged, with his blond-grey hair cropped short. He walked in front of the Jeep and took down my license plate number, and then came over to my open window.

"I'm here to visit my father." I smiled at him.

"May I see both of your driver's licenses?"

I slid mine out of my wallet and Michael handed me his, and I gave them to the officer. He copied down the information and handed back the licenses.

"I'll be right back sir. Stay in your car." He walked into the building.

"Are you okay? I mean, are you scared?" Michael lifted one of his legs, bent it under him, and sat on his foot like a restless child.

"Of course I'm anxious, but I'm ready to see him."

The guard walked back to the Jeep. "I'm sorry sir, but neither of you are on the list today."

"What list?"

"The list of visitors approved to go beyond this point." He looked at me, surprised. "You didn't fill out a visitor request form?"

"No. I didn't know I had to." I felt as stupid as Michael had earlier implied.

The guard handed me a clipboard connected to a pen by a chain. "Here. Fill this out. Someone from our information officer's office will call you in a few days." I could see him watching me as I filled out the form. "You say you're the inmate's son, right?" I nodded my head as I continued writing. "So your approval should happen pretty quick, probably a couple days." The guard looked at the clear sky overhead. "Did you have to drive through any rain, coming out? I heard Round Rock had three inches last night. Can you believe it, at this time of year?" He noticed I had finished and took the clipboard from me. "I'll get this to processing today. By the way, your friend won't be able to get in when you come back."

I turned the Jeep around in the small gravel lot near the guard station, causing a cloud of white dust, and headed back toward Austin.

"Don't even say it." I looked at Michael, who sat fidgeting in his seat. "You were right, I wasn't thinking."

"It's no big deal. Like you said, I didn't have anything else to do today. Anyway, now you know the drill. You'll be able to see him in a few days."

"I may not even come back. Maybe driving out here and filling out that form was enough."

"Are you for real? You're so fucking fickle, Thorpe. I thought you wanted to reconnect with your dad. Like you said, he's the only family you have left. But what the hell, most times I think you don't even know what you want."

"You know what I want?" I looked into the rearview mirror and then toward Michael." I want to see Copper One."

"I thought you were going to come up with a new name."

"I will, but I haven't given it much thought yet. Besides, I think it would help if I could actually see it." I smiled at him. "I'm serious. Can we stop by your studio when we get home?"

"Sure, but I'm not totally finished. I postponed the symphony guy because I'm still unsure about the sounds I want the wind openings to make." Michael looked out the side window for a minute before turning back toward me. "But it *looks* finished. Once it's tuned, I'm going to mount it on that slab of caramel colored marble I bought in Cuernavaca last year."

"Then what'll you do with it?"

"Have some slides taken, and then try to get a gallery to take it."

"What about that guy we met at Laguna Gloria?" I couldn't believe I was bringing him up.

"Oh, him. That guy turned out to be a big loser. I met with him a few weeks ago and you were right. He *was* more interested in me than my work."

"That's too bad."

"Yeah, I was pretty pissed. But I slept with him anyway."

I jerked my head toward Michael and took my foot off the accelerator for a moment.

"What?" Michael looked at me confused.

"I'm just surprised, that's all." I sped up and kept my eyes on the road. "You just said he was a loser and led you on about being interested in your work . . . ."

"I know, but he was sort of cute, and I hadn't had sex with anyone for a long time." Michael yawned. "He said he wanted to see me again but I haven't called him."

"Why not?" I felt relieved.

"I think he's a jerk. Plus, the sex wasn't that exciting, but it *was* sex, after all." He looked at me, smiling. "You know, it's like that old joke. Sex is like pizza. When it's good, it's really, really good. But when it's bad, it's still okay."

I turned to him and smiled, not yet ready to laugh.

"And okay was good enough at the time. But you know— and maybe I feel this way because I've grown up a bit since Houston—I like to at least have some sort of heart connection when I'm with someone, even if it's a stranger. Otherwise . . . well, otherwise, I'd just rather jerk off."

I swallowed hard and nodded like I understood.

"What about you? You doing anyone lately?"

"I haven't felt horny in months. Maybe something's really wrong with me. I think I've become asexual."

"Yeah, right. Whatever happened to that lovely architect Lexy said you were seeing right before I moved back to Austin?"

"Oh, Meridian. Well, I did like her a lot. She was a lot of fun, but we didn't go out for very long."

"What happened?"

"Well, let's put it this way." I turned to Michael and smiled. "I never even tasted the pizza."

Michael threw his head back and began laughing. I took the Riverside exit and rolled down my window to breathe in the fresh coolness of Town Lake, glad that we were home.

"So anyway, you got any other prospects? For Copper One, I mean."

"Well, I was talking to Lexy the other day and she told me that she had just found out about a local foundation that supports Austin artists."

"Great."

"Not so great. The deadline for submitting the grant proposal was July 15."

"That was almost a month ago."

"*Exactamundo*, buddy."

"It still sounds like a good idea, though, for next year. You need to get more of your stuff in public."

"I know. Lexy's getting me a copy of the guidelines." Michael sighed. "I really think Copper One, or whatever we decide to call it, will be my best piece yet, once I settle on the right sounds."

* * *

The phone was ringing as I opened the door to my house. I let the machine get it. "Hello, David. This is Helen Moody. I was just a little concerned and thought I'd call. When you didn't come by on Tuesday, I didn't think much of it. But when you didn't show again today, I started to worry. Please call me when you get in."

I opened the kitchen door to let Abby in the house. She allowed me to pet her for a moment before running into the living room and bringing back her rope toy. She sat on her haunches and taunted me with one of the knotted ends of the toy. I tugged at it halfheartedly for a moment and then let go.

"I'm sorry, Ab. Daddy doesn't want to play now. Go chew it up." She continued to nuzzle the toy against my hand as I stood next to the stove, but I refused to grab it, and after a minute she dropped it at my feet and walked away.

I filled the kettle on the stove with water and turned on the flame, and then spooned a mixture of dried valerian root and chamomile blossoms into the white porcelain teapot on the counter.

On the cookbook shelf I noticed the mahogany box I had brought from Aunt Ivy's house. In it, she had saved scraps of paper: recipes from neighbors and old friends, newspaper clippings, gardening notes. It had also collected stray buttons, wide bobby pins and pennies. After having transferred most of her things into a manila envelope, I had been using the hand-size box like she had, except in addition to papers, it now contained rubber bands, paper clips and quarters.

I turned down the flame under the kettle and took the box from the shelf. I reached to the bottom and pulled out the faded newspaper clippings that I had kept in various places since my father was sent to prison. I held them up to my face and breathed in the dusty scent and felt the grainy, yellowed pulp of the paper. The first article had appeared on the first page of the Metro Section of the San Antonio Express and was dated March 12, 1976:

"A San Antonio man was killed yesterday afternoon by a single shotgun blast to the chest near Medina Lake in what appears to be a hunting accident.

"Bob Grimes, 24, of northwest San Antonio was pronounced dead by Sgt. Alex Mendoza of the Bexar County Sheriff's Department, which is investigating the incident. Mendoza said Grimes had been duck hunting near the lake with a co-worker, David Thorpe, Sr., 36, also of San Antonio, when the incident occurred.

"Mendoza said the incident has been ruled an accident, but further investigation will be conducted. Thorpe was held for questioning and released."

I put the clipping back in the box and read the second one which was dated a week later:

"David Thorpe, Sr., 36, of northeast San Antonio, has been arrested for the murder of Bob Grimes. Grimes, an associate of Thorpe's in the San Antonio accounting firm of Haskins and McConnell, was killed earlier this month during what was first thought to be a hunting accident.

"Bexar County Sheriff's spokeswoman Margaret Lovage reported that Thorpe was taken into custody, booked and released on $50,000 bond pending his trial to be set for sometime in May. Lovage said the bond amount reflects the fact that Thorpe is a low flight risk."

The tea kettle went off with a high whistle, startling me. I turned off the flame and poured more than half of the water from the kettle into the teapot and replaced the lid. I closed my eyes for a few minutes and let the tea steep before filling an oversized mug. The hot tea felt soothing to my throat and stomach. I sat on one of the stools next to the kitchen counter and continued reading the news clipping.

"The Express News has learned that Thorpe was the subject of an embezzling investigation earlier this year at the accounting firm that employed him. Robert McConnell, managing partner of Haskins and McConnell, where Thorpe remains employed on unpaid leave, confirmed that Thorpe had been a person of interest in the incident involving the apparent theft of half a million dollars from the firm. However, McConnell said Thorpe was cleared of the crime when an outside investigator discovered that a computer error was the actual culprit."

I refilled my mug with tea and read part of the last newspaper article I had saved:

"David Thorpe, Sr., 36, was convicted yesterday in U.S. District court of manslaughter in the death of Bob Grimes, which occurred in east Bexar County on March 11 of this year. Thorpe will immediately begin serving a 20-year sentence in the state penitentiary in Huntsville."

I put the articles back into the box and set it on the shelf. I sat there, on the counter in the brightness of my nighttime kitchen, and finished drinking the pot of tea.

My phone's ringing broke the silence of my sleep the next morning, jangling me into consciousness.

"Hello." The receiver felt cold against my cheek, which was warm and damp from being pressed against a pillow.

"Mr. Thorpe?" a woman's voice spoke.

"Yeah," I rolled over on my back, rubbing my eyes.

"Mr. Thorpe, this is officer Cannon in the visitor processing office at the State Correctional Facility in Huntsville." I looked at the clock next to my bed and it read nine-thirty. I pulled the covers up to my head and my heart began to beat faster. "I'm calling in regard to a visitor request form I received from you about seeing your father."

"Yes?"

"Well, sir. I have good news for you. Well, I hope it's good anyway. Your father has been released."

"What do you mean he's been released?"

"I'm looking at his records now, and it looks like he served more than half his sentence, which is actually more than most. He was assigned to a halfway house in Taylor, under the supervision of a parole officer."

"You mean Tyler, right, not Taylor?" I thought she must have meant Tyler, the larger city north of Huntsville in East Texas.

"I meant what I said: Taylor." She sounded annoyed. "It's east of Round Rock, near Austin."

I took a drink from the water glass sitting on my nightstand. "I'm sorry. I was just confused. Could you give me the address of the place in Taylor?" I picked up the pencil and pad of paper near my alarm clock.

"Sure." I heard the woman tapping on a computer keyboard, "But he wouldn't still be there, sir. That was over two years ago. Even his parole supervision period has ended by now. He's a free man, he could be anywhere."

My heart jumped through my chest as the phone receiver fell from my hand, onto my bed where it slid along the bedspread and then down onto the floor, from where I heard a woman's faint voice for a few seconds, followed by a couple of clicks and then the continual throb of an off-the-hook tone.

7

"Mr. Goetz will be right with you, Mr. Thorpe. Please hold." I heard Goetz's secretary press the dial pad, and a Bach concerto played softly as I waited. In the middle of a lengthy crescendo, Goetz picked up the phone.

"David, hello. How are you?"

"I'm fine, but I need your help." I was talking on my cordless phone, pacing between my living room and the kitchen.

"Concerning what, something about Mrs. Schumann's estate?"

"No. I want you to help me locate my father."

"Is he not in prison in Huntsville?"

"That's what I thought, but I just found out earlier this morning that he's been released. He was let out two years ago."

"Are you positive?"

"I'm sure."

"Did the prison contact you?"

"Yes, but only because I tried to see him."

"When did all this happen?"

"I drove out to Huntsville with a friend of mine last week and . . . it's a long story and I don't want to get into it right now, but the point is I found out he's out and now I want to find him. I can't believe no one tried to notify me when he was let out."

"Well, this is certainly big news. How much of his sentence did he serve?"

"Almost fifteen of twenty, which I now know is a lot, but I never really thought about the possibility of his being released. He was on parole after he left Huntsville, but supposedly that's even expired. Listen, Friedreich, if the prison had been of any more help, I wouldn't be bothering you."

"It's okay, David. My firm is here to help. Do you think your father tried to find you when he got out?"

"I admit I'm sort of rattled about this. I don't know what I think, but I know I don't think that. I'm easy to find. I can't imagine it would be very difficult to find someone, unless they don't want to be found—and I didn't not want to be found!"

"Slow down, David. You do seem flustered. Actually, considering the circumstances, you sound quite calm. Are you sure about wanting to find him? I'm just thinking that you haven't had contact with the man in fifteen years, and, well, he was convicted of murder, after all."

"He didn't try to kill *me*. *I'm* not afraid of him. Besides, if he had wanted to find me, he could have. That's my point, Friedreich, he doesn't *want* to find me."

"You're right; you probably have nothing to fear."

"I know I don't. I just want to find out where he's living. It unnerves me knowing he's out there, somewhere. I just want your firm to find him, that's all."

"Did the warden's office say where he was released to?"

"I got the address to a halfway house in Taylor, though the woman I talked to said he's long gone by now."

"Good. I mean that's okay. It's a start. What else do you know?"

"Nothing."

"That's fine. We'll begin by getting his social security number from police records and go from there."

"Friedreich?" I sat down on the couch next to the base for the cordless phone.

"Yes, David."

"How difficult, really, is it to find someone?"

"Well, it's hard to say. My associate Barry Bristow handles most of our criminal cases. He works with PIs all the time and says they can pretty much find anyone. But your previous point was a good one." He paused and I heard him take a breath. "When someone doesn't want to be found, it can make the task all the more difficult."

"The cost doesn't concern me."

"I know, David. We'll find him. You may have to be patient, that's all."

"Do you want me to do anything in the mean time?"

"Try to relax. Why don't you go spend a healthy chunk of that inheritance. You'd be surprised at how much fun you can have."

* * *

"I'm here to see Lexy Jameson." I stood in front of a reception desk on the third floor of the LBJ Presidential Library, looking down at a woman who had stopped thumbing through a thick fashion magazine.

"Do you have an appointment?" The young woman slid a file folder over the magazine, which had lain open to a full-page perfume ad.

"No, but she'll see me."

"And your name?"

"No, don't buzz her, please. I want to surprise her."

"Ms. Jameson doesn't like surprises."

"Trust me, she won't mind. I'm an old friend." I walked past her desk and opened Lexy's office door, which had been ajar and noiselessly walked in. She was leaning back in a large chair upholstered in brown leather, talking on the phone with her eyes closed.

"No, Marcy. Cut back on the catering budget if you have to, but don't skimp on the flowers. Lady Bird Johnson's going to be there, remember? I want lots of flowers, big showy arrangements, you understand? And not just any flowers, I want them to be absolutely exquisite. Don't let me down."

Lexy shook her head rhythmically as if she were willing the person on the other line to stop speaking. "Sounds good. Okay, Marcy, fine. I've got to go. Let's meet in my office tomorrow afternoon, say twoish, to finalize the details." Lexy hung up the phone and sighed, her eyes still closed.

"Geez, I'm glad I don't work for you."

Lexy turned and opened her eyes, startled. "Jesus, David. You scared me. What're you doing here?"

"Nada—besides listening to you intimidate the hell out of some poor soul, what was her name, Marcy?" I smiled.

"She's a big girl, she can take care of herself. So really, what's up?"

"Just stopped by to say hi and see if you wanted to take an early lunch." I sat in one of the two padded chairs angled in front of her desk.

"God, I'd love to, but I've got a luncheon meeting with the Library Board in half an hour about the fund raiser." Lexy ran her fingers through her hair and then rubbed two of them on her left earlobe next to a large gold earring. "I'll never forgive Mrs. Delgado for dumping this godforsaken project on me."

"Stop thinking of it like that. You're sending it negative energy."

"The problem is that it's sapping all of *my* energy. Next month's newsletter *and* the annual report are running behind because of it."

"Oh Lexy, come on. You live for chaos."

"Not like this. Production schedules and printer deadlines are one thing, but I hate all this event planning crap." She sipped from a coffee mug that had been sitting on a stack of papers fanned across her desk, leaned back in her chair and smiled. "Oh well, I could bitch all day so I won't. I'm sorry. So what's going on?"

"I'm thinking about spending some money."

"Oh yeah?" Lexy leaned forward in her chair and smiled. "What for?"

"I'm not sure. I thought I'd start with lunch for two at Les Amis, but since you can't go, I think I'll go to the mall and buy some new clothes."

Lexy began clapping. "Good idea. Take Michael with you. Even if he doesn't have the money to buy much, he does have good taste in clothes.

"And *I* don't?" I pretended to act indignant.

"You could stand to look a little less like a dirt farmer."

"I'd rather go alone. Besides, Michael's meeting with that symphony guy to tune his sculpture today."

"He's finally been inspired?"

"Guess so. He's being sort of closed-mouthed about it though. Oh well, I know you're busy, so I guess I'll take off."

"I wish I could skip out to have lunch and go shopping with you, but there's just no way. We should get together this weekend, maybe go to Barton Springs."

"Yeah, that'd be good." I stood to leave.

"Why don't you walk across campus to the Drag and have that lunch at Les Amis. There's no law against dining alone. Plus, there's even a new men's clothing store near Twenty-fourth. You should check it out."

"I don't know, Lex. I think I'll just go on to the mall."

"Actually, David, I'm trying to be manipulative. I have a favor to ask. See that box?" Lexy pointed to the credenza behind her desk next to a droopy dieffenbachia. "The printer just delivered it a few minutes ago. It's the VIP invitations to the gala. I wanted my assistant to deliver them before noon to the UT president's office for him to sign, but she's got a dentist appointment." She looked at me and batted her eyelashes. "Would you be a dear and deliver them for me? I'll owe you."

"Sure, what the hell." I walked over to the credenza, broke off a few yellow leaves on the dieffenbachia, and picked up the box. "This poor thing could use some water. Would you mind?"

"I'll water it as soon as you leave, I promise. Thanks so much for doing this for me. You're a doll. You do know where to go, right? In the Main Building, tenth floor . . . ."

"Yeah, yeah." I walked toward the door.

"And, David?" Lexy had stood up from her chair and walked me to the door. She handed me a glossy tri-fold brochure.   "Here's some information on the Library's charitable foundation and some community projects its supporting. Since you're still looking for ways to spend some of your inheritance, I thought you might see something that interests you." She winked at me. "Procuring a hefty donation just might get me a big fat raise."

"Anything else, Lex? How about a brand new Porsche?"

"Make it a BMW and we've got a deal." Lexy smiled and hugged me briefly and then pulled back. "Have fun at the mall. Try Scarbrough's. They already have their fall line in and are probably having a summer clearance sale." *As if*, I thought, but only returned her smile and nodded.

I took the elevator to the ground floor and walked toward the library's main entrance. A portrait of LBJ loomed between two sets of thick glass doors. I glanced up at it and couldn't help but think that the grandfatherly figure posed inside the gilded frame was somehow forcing me to walk in the shadow of the Tower to drop off his invitations.

I passed through one of the doors and took the steps two at a time.   I crossed Trinity Street and continued toward Memorial Stadium and the East Mall fountain, passing by the Performing Arts Center and the Fine Arts Library. All the buildings appeared new on the east side of campus. The large, grassy expanses gave the whole area a park like feel. I headed toward a sidewalk shaded by oak trees to escape the midday August sun. As I continued west, the trees became larger and the buildings appeared more imposing and sat closer together. I walked up the steps between Garrison and Welch halls, toward the older part of campus. My stomach knotted as I closed in on the Tower, and my legs felt heavy. I hadn't been on that part of campus in years; but seeing the same red tile roofed buildings, the same stately trees and carefully trimmed boxwood hedges had the effect of making me feel as if I never left. And within a minute of stepping onto the Main Mall I was standing at the base of the Tower with the box of invitations under my arm, looking up at the inscription, trembling.

In the beginning, I didn't even know it was from the Bible, though the first two words should've clued me in. Carved in a field of cream colored granite, the message loomed above the Mall on the base of UT's clock tower, reading, "Ye shall know the truth and the truth shall make you free."

I had first read the line during freshman orientation ten years earlier. After a day of meetings on everything from how to use the Undergraduate Library to the art of properly telling an Aggie joke, Michael and I, as good little Longhorn wannabes, had stayed on to take the campus tour. An upperclassman geek served as guide, his shtick honed from weeks of freshman tours. When our group stopped at the statues surrounding the South Mall, the stretch of lawn that framed the view of the state capitol, he enthusiastically started in about the George Washington likeness that stood facing downtown. "And if you look at him from the side . . . ." The guide herded our small group to an angle in the director of Batts Hall and pointed to the large bronze hand that held the erect handle of the sword sheathed at the statue's waist. ". . . It looks like ol' George had a good grip on things when he posed for this one, eh?" A self-satisfied grin spread across the guide's face. He then moved to the back of the statue and pointed to the dedication plaque. "See, *'Erected* by the Texas Society of the Daughters of the American Revolution.'" Michael and I laughed, thinking it was funny even though the geek's delivery was lame.

The guide then led the group up the steps onto the Main Mall, explaining, "Now, about the clock tower. Of course you all know about the sniper incident of 1966, during which Charles Whitman holed himself up on the observation deck and picked off twelve victims before he was snubbed out by a SWAT team from San Antonio. It was the darkest day in UT history, and the observation deck has been closed to visitors ever since." I looked up at the deck hundreds of feet above, and imagined the sniper perched with his rifles. "But anyway," the guide sounded almost cheery as he directed our group farther west, toward the Student Union Building, and pointed up to the clock tower that rose from the observation deck, "if you look at it from this angle, it looks like an owl. See." He pointed toward the two visible clock faces. "The dials become eyes and the corner of the deck is the beak." He went on to explain that it was an intentional resemblance, because the architect was a Rice U. graduate and the owl his alma mater's mascot. And it did look like an owl, but I was more impressed with the huge brass encircled clocks. The hands stood at six o'clock as the cathedral like chimes began playing the tune to the first line of "The Eyes of Texas Are Upon You," which is basically the same as "I've Been Working on the Railroad." After the music stopped, there were six resolute gongs. And, as I lowered my eyes from the south-facing clock I saw the words, all at once and then as a sentence: "Ye shall know the truth and the truth shall make you free."

From that day on I always read the words when I walked across campus, but I seldom allowed myself to think about them for very long, always in a hurry to get somewhere, anywhere. Eventually I became convinced that the tower was speaking directly to me. I was ye, and it frightened me. By junior year it had started to eat at me so much that I would walk all the way around the Main Building to get to the Union, just to avoid passing in front of the Tower and its personal prescription.

The package of invitations grew heavy under my arm, and as I continued walking toward the doors of the Main Building, the words and the Tower disappeared above me. I ran up the steps, opened one of the heavy doors, and took the elevator to the tenth floor. I gave the box to the president's secretary. I left the building on the side facing the Union and walked through the patio area toward the Drag, stopping to look at the coins scattered in the shallow bowl of Peace Fountain. Some were old and dull; others were glistening in the wavy sunlight. An overweight pigeon with a purple and green sheen to its feathers noisily landed on the fountain's edge. It seemed to stare me down and made me feel unwelcome. I decided to skip the Drag and walk back across campus, taking a different route, to the LBJ Library parking lot.

I stopped at my bank and withdrew a large amount of cash before driving to Barton Creek Mall. I wandered through the open space between the stores, looking at the people and feeling empowered at being disconnected from them, especially those with children in tow. Their lives were complicated, I thought. I could do whatever I wanted, whenever I wanted. Feeling aloof and arrogant I moved aimlessly through the mall.

I walked into a place called The Terrace Cafe and sat at one of many empty glass topped tables. I got an iced tea and sipped it, looking at the people gathering in the distance around a large fountain with four levels of waterfalls. I could hear the splashing in spite of high pitched voices echoing through the large, captured space. I remembered how I had once wanted to wade into a similar fountain when I was a young boy shopping with my mom at Central Park Mall in San Antonio. I had told her I wanted to pick out the pennies. She knelt and opened her purse and searched out stray pennies to give me. "Here, David. Make a few wishes," she said. I threw the pennies one at a time into the shallow pool. She came up behind me and put her hands on my shoulders when I was finished. "When those pennies settled to the bottom, they became your wishes. Now, you wouldn't want some other little boy to come along, wade into the water, and take away *your* wishes, would you?" She gently rubbed my back and smiled.

I left my waiter a ten dollar bill for the tea and continued ambling throughout the mall. I ended up at Pet World. The two Dalmatian puppies in the window had been an adorable draw. They looked like twins and reminded me of Freckles, who had been a present from Mom and Dad for my fifth birthday. I wanted to be behind the glass playing with them. Before I knew it, I had become sucked into heartbreak row: the stacks of chrome wire cages that enclosed the rest of the store's puppies, most sleeping, several yelping, in the bright light of their cell block. I forced myself to move quickly past them, deciding to get a cart, which I then pushed toward the product aisles.

The cart squeaked as I wheeled it through the store, which appeared surreally lit by too many fluorescent bulbs. I stopped in the middle of the dog product aisle, pausing to stare into the deep cavity of my empty cart. The racks were full of squeaky plastic toys, rawhide bones of all sizes, brightly colored rubber rings and balls, and assorted dog treats.

I noticed other customers moving down the aisle, pausing to select an item or two before moving on, appearing confident they had made the right choices. The bright light and loud colors made my head pound, and I began to perspire. My headache soon faded and I smiled at a young girl passing by toward the aquariums at the back of the store. I selected a yellow and green knobby ball that squeaked as I grabbed it. I liked the sound and squeezed it several times, smiling, before tossing it into my basket. That ball wouldn't last a day before Abby chewed it to shreds, I thought, so I emptied the racks of all the other color combinations of similar balls and other squeaky shapes like bones and rolled newspapers. I began to empty each rack methodically as quickly as I could. I hung all the rubber rings onto my arms like bracelets and then flung them one by one into the basket. I dumped the bins of rawhide bones and other shapes, natural and basted, into my basket before emptying higher shelves of Cheweez snacks, milk bones, "Roxanne's Gourmet Scone Bones," and flavored bottled waters "for the discriminating canine palate." The broth flavors sounded gross to me, so I opted for strawberry and kiwi because Abby seemed to like most fruits. I pushed the filled cart up toward the front of the store and grabbed another one.

I filled the second cart, clearing out most of the remaining toys. I grabbed all the Frisbees and sailed each of them into the cart before emptying the hangers of knotted rope toys. I added six leather leashes of different lengths and four twenty-pound bags of the store's best dog food, two beef flavor, one bacon and cheese, and one lamb. I pushed the cart to my first one, and then pushed and pulled both of them to a cash register aisle. The middle-aged woman behind the counter had the name "Margie" on a bone-shaped gold tag pinned to her turquoise blue Pet World vest. She was overweight and her vest hung open over a tightly stretched, white double-knit blouse.

"Did you find everything all right, sir?" She smiled and then whispered, "The dog food is going to go on sale tomorrow. I could hold it for you if you want."

"Thanks, but that's okay. I'll just take everything now."

"I know that stuff is expensive, so I try to help people out whenever I can." She looked at the full, unattended basket behind me. "Is that yours, too?"

"Yeah, is that a problem?"

"Not at all. Is this going to be cash, check or charge?"

"Cash."

"Are you a breeder?" Margie began scanning the price of each item, looking up at me.

"No, I don't think I could ever do that." I pulled my wallet out of my back pocket.

"Because I was going to say if you were, well, you could be buying this stuff at our warehouse store on South Lamar, near William Cannon Boulevard. You'd need to buy a membership card and everything, though."

After ringing up my total and looking at it closely, she turned to me and smiled. "I don't mean to be nosey, but how many dogs *do* you have?"

"Oh, only one." I looked at the floor.

Soon after Lexy had moved back from New York several years earlier, she decided to start a fitness regimen that included walking three mornings a week along Town Lake. She had made me come with her early that first Saturday morning in early January. The sun had just come up and it was miserably cold, the temperature hovering around fifteen degrees, wind whipping sleet with occasional snow, which was quite rare for Central Texas.

She had knocked on my door before seven o'clock, appearing so bundled up that I could only see the center of her face: a nose, a lip and the bottom halves of two green eyes. I put on my down jacket and brown leather gloves.

"Are you sure you still want to do this?" I hadn't given up on trying to dissuade her. "You know, I could go get coffee and low-fat muffins at Sweetish Hill and we could just stay in and watch cartoons."

"Come on, let's go. If I don't start today, I may never do it. I need you, David. Let's just go. It'll warm up."

We walked down the slope of Ninth Street, gingerly, as to avoid sliding on the ice. The large pecan trees were merely a lattice of limbs, hung with ice. We followed Lamar to the river and followed a trail toward the old warehouse district south of downtown. Everything was deserted. There was no one else senseless enough to be out, I thought. Sure it'll warm up, my ass.

"Isn't this great?" Lexy twirled ahead of me, her outstretched arms brushing against dormant willow branches hung thick with icicles.

"It's fucking cold as hell." I pulled the brim of my felt baseball cap down and moved my shoulders up and down.

"Hell's not cold, David. How many times do I have to point that out?" Lexy bounced along the trail and I imagined her having visions of calories melting in her head. She stopped a few yards in front of me and pulled off her ear muffs. "What's that noise?"

"What noise?" I caught up with her and followed her toward the river bank, crackling through the straw like brush.

"Over here. Listen." Lexy stopped and I stood still and we heard a muffled whimper. "Oh David, look. It's a puppy. My God, he's wet with mud." Lexy crouched to pick up the reddish-brown thing from the newspapers and trash strewn in the frozen undergrowth near the water's edge. "Why would anyone do this? Oh David, he's just a baby." Lexy held the dog up and away from her a bit. "It's a little girl, oh God, David, unzip your coat." Lexy tucked the pup into my jacket, smearing mud on the new flannel shirt Aunt Ivy had given me that Christmas, then closed the zipper part way. She gave the puppy a kiss on it's tiny black nose and said, "Everything will be all right. Yes it will, I promise."

We ran the rest of the way home. Lexy rambled on about why anyone would do such a thing. She speculated on how long the puppy had been there. It couldn't have been long, she reasoned, not long at all. But why—she kept talking, fast to keep up with our movement—why take it all the way down to the river? Surely it couldn't have wandered there on its own. No, someone must have dumped her, she concluded. I'd never seen Lexy so frantic or so upset. We reached my house within fifteen minutes.

Lexy bathed the puppy in warm water, removing the clotted mud from her fur, and then dried her with a towel that I had draped over the radiator. After lapping two small bowls of milk the puppy fell asleep against a pillow on my bed.

Lexy told me she had always wanted a dog, but it wouldn't be fair to keep her because she didn't have a yard, and the puppy was going to be big. "Did you notice those feet?" she asked.

It didn't take much for her to convince me to keep the dog. I had been hoping that she would want me to have her.

"We should name her Abigail." Lexy sounded resolute as we sat on the bed watching the puppy sleep.

"Abigail?" I kept my voice low. "After your imaginary sister?"

"She was real enough to me at the time, okay? I think it would be an appropriate honor."

"For someone who never existed?"

Lexy signed and looked at me pleadingly.

"Good, okay, Abigail. I like it." I reached out and petted the sleeping mass of fur and swollen stomach. "Abby, our little foundling, has found herself a home."

I noticed that my porch light had burned out when I pulled into my driveway, making me feel unwelcome at my own home. I carried all the bags of Pet World stuff into the living room and dumped them in piles on the rug in front of the couch before I let Abby in from the backyard. She bounded through the kitchen and into the living room. I calmed her down with petting and attention, and held her by her collar as she began to notice the things behind me.

I held her head between my hands and pointed her face toward mine. "Yes ma'am, little monkey girl, it's all for you. Go play, you big monk." I kissed her snout and let her go. She ran toward the packages, sniffing at all the stuff, her tail wagging hard. She looked at me, as if she needed assurance that everything was indeed for her. I petted her around her head and neck and then I opened each package as if I were being timed, until we were surrounded by mounds of dog toys and treats—all nine hundred and eighty-four dollars worth. Cardboard and plastic packaging lay strewn across the rug in front of the couch and under the coffee table, looking like Christmas morning in a household with a dozen children. Abby nosed through the debris and picked up a red Frisbee. She came up to me, the Frisbee hanging from her lower canines, and dropped it in front of me. I patted her head. "Not in the house, Ab. Here." I handed her a knobby squeaky toy. "Go ahead, chew it up." She lay in front of me and muffled squeaks disappeared when she ripped a gash in the rubber ball. I handed her another and rolled the silenced one under the couch.

In spite of Pet World, a ten dollar iced tea, and buying my house from my landlord a month before, I couldn't believe I still had more than five million dollars left. Abby walked away from the pile of toys, carrying a small rawhide bone in her mouth, and lay next to me on the couch. She chewed the bone, holding it upright between her paws. After a while, she sat up on her haunches, closer to me, and we both looked at everything scattered across the room. And we just sat there together, dumbfounded, quite overwhelmed by it all.

8

Mrs. **Moody walked through the weathered** picket gate
separating her front and side yards from the back. Her face was
pink from the sun and she was wearing long canvas shorts that
reached below her knees and a white, short-sleeved blouse.

"Well, how do the front beds look?" I glanced up at her
from where I was standing, in the middle of the crescent shaped
trench I had just finished digging for a water garden. My t-shirt,
shorts and sneakers were covered with dirt.

"As good as we can expect at this time of year." She latched
the gate and walked over to me. "We'll sure have our work cut
out for us this fall. Everything has become so thick, especially
that yarrow." She shook her head. "It's lovely, but boy does it
spread. I'd like to clean out that bed and move most of the
plants back here so we have room to plant bulbs in the front.
I've never had much luck with them, though. My narcissus
seems to do well, but I'd like something else with a little more
color, like tulips. Do you know much about planting bulbs,
David?"

"It's not a big deal. I used to help my Aunt Ivy divide and
replant hers each fall. You just wait 'til it gets cool, and then
work some bone meal into the soil and stick 'em in, fairly deep
for tulips."

"You make everything sound so easy."

"It is easy. You know, Helen, I'm planning on doing some work on my aunt's yard next month and I'll be dividing the bulbs. I can get you a whole bed full of tulips for free, if you want them."

"Oh David, that would be wonderful. What color are they?"

"They're all red, well, more of a crimson color."

"Perfect. I love deep reds."

"Yeah, they're pretty intense. Aunt Ivy ordered them directly from this specialty grower in Holland in the late '70s. They're called Resurrection Blaze."

"The name alone sounds pretty intense. I can hardly wait until spring." Mrs. Moody surveyed the three-foot-deep trench. "My, you've sure earned your keep today, just look at you." Dirt clung to the hair on my legs and arms and I was dripping with sweat in the late August heat.

"Yeah, I'm pretty beat. I'm going to drive out to Lake Travis to cool off when I'm done here."

"That sounds like a fine idea." Her eyes widened and she smiled. "When we were young, Dr. Moody and I loved to drive out to Lake Travis for a swim. It's so beautiful and peaceful in places, but I hear it can get pretty crowded these days."

"Maybe on the weekends. But it should be pretty deserted today." I pushed away the matted hair that hung past my eyebrows and wiped my forehead. "So, are you all ready for your big birthday bash next week?"

"Oh yes, I'm even starting to get enthusiastic about it. I know it's only my bridge club, but I've decided to go all out with the food. I'm having it catered by LaSalle's."

"Great idea. Why put yourself through all that work?" I shoveled the last of the loose dirt from the trench.

"That's what I thought. You know, I've been thinking about what you said a few months ago about seventy-five not being that old . . . ."

"Good, because it's not. Look at you; you're the picture of health." I scraped the caked-on dirt from the shovel blade with my shoe.

"Now David, you're exaggerating. I know I could stand to lose a few pounds, and then there's my back, of course. But I'm thinking of this birthday as a new beginning, so I want it to be extra special. They say aging is all in your mind." She fanned her face with her hands. "Oh David, I almost forgot. Before you go I want to show you something." She motioned me to follow her.

I'd never seen her walk so quickly as she led me to her greenhouse, a wood frame and glass building next to the garage. Inside, on a small shelf next to an open window, sat a shallow plastic planting tray. She pointed to several four-leaved seedlings standing an inch tall. "It's the mountain laurel seeds you brought me. I'm transplanting them next week, on the morning of my birthday. Isn't this exciting?" Mrs. Moody's smile faded and she looked up at my face as she gently gripped my forearms. "David, I'm a sentimental old fool sometimes, but I just wanted to tell you how happy I am that you're a part of my life. You are a dear, dear boy." She again smiled and her eyes welled up. "I hope you find someone who'll make you as happy as my Randolph made me. I miss him so much."

* * *

I turned into the new parking area the county had built to prevent the weekend line of cars that had once stretched along the narrow road. There were only a handful of cars in the lot. I grabbed my pack from the back seat and followed the asphalt trail that connected the parking lot to two public rest rooms, and eventually, to the lower gravel trails that wound among the rocks at the lake's shore. Near the beginning of the main trail, a small brown sign with white lettering read, "If nudity offends you, do not pass beyond this point."

I walked along the crushed limestone trail, which was bordered by thick scrub oak and juniper. I'd never seen the shore so empty of sunbathers. I saw only two women, lying naked in the sun on their backs with their eyes closed. I continued on a hundred yards past them, winding among the huge granite boulders that appeared as if frozen in mid tumble into the clear lake. The breeze was even too slight to disturb the water's surface, and I could see a yellow sailboat, so far in the distance that I could hide it from my sight with an outstretched hand.

I found a flat slab of rock and unhooked my pack from my shoulder, unzipped it, and pulled out an oversized bath towel. I spread it on the rock and looked around, noticing that I was no longer within sight of the women. I took off my shoes and socks, shaking the dirt onto the ground next to my rock. I stripped off my sweaty t-shirt, looked around one more time, and then stood up and pulled off my shorts and underwear. There were borders of clean skin at my waistline, and where my socks had ended partway up my calves. It felt good being in the hot sun without any clothes. I walked to the water's edge, stood on a low outcropping, and dove shallow, just skimming the surface. I swam toward the deep water. When I was out fifty yards or so, I stopped swimming and treaded water while I took in the view. The secluded stretch of rocky shoreline curved inward to create the cove that was Hippie Hollow. I could hardly see the two women. I rubbed my arms and legs under the water to remove any traces of dirt.

I felt like a dolphin as I continued to swim away from the shore, diving deep, feeling the cool water glide over my torso, causing the beginnings of hard-on. I did back-flips at the surface, taking a breath with each one, before again diving deep into the clear blue water. More than cleaning off the day's accumulation of sweat and dirt, I was taking the water into my body, enjoying its tugging at my soul. At that moment I not only wanted to act like a dolphin, I really wanted to be one, communicating differently, separated from the limits of earth.

I didn't know how long I had been out in the lake when my leg began to cramp, reminding me that I was unfortunately indeed human after all and needed to get back to shore. I swam, alternating various strokes until my leg loosened up, and stopped when I could stand waist-deep. I looked down and saw that I was still partially hard, bobbing at the water's surface. I continued walking out of the lake and sat on my sun-warmed towel. I sat with my arms wrapped around my legs, which were bent at the knees, and my erection subsided as I sat drying, looking out over the water. My breathing slowed, and I felt clean and renewed.

I pulled out a brown bottle of suntan oil from my pack, poured from it into my cupped palm, and rubbed the coconut scented oil over my body. Feeling relaxed and content, I lay back and closed my eyes, fantasizing that I was lying on a secluded Mexican beach, and dozed off.

"Say, you're getting pretty red there, guy. You ought to turn over and let your ass get some of this fabulous sunshine." The voice pierced my sleep and I woke, dazed as to where I was. I quickly turned over and looked up, blinking into the bright sun, at the young man who had spoken to me. He stood on the rock next to mine, wearing a black Speedo and holding a towel.

"Hi, I'm Mick. Sorry to startle you, but that sun would've broiled your balls if you didn't turn over."

"Thanks." I rubbed at my eyes. He looked about twenty-one, about my height, but with a dark tan and a lean, hairless body more defined than mine. I was turned on by his bright eyes and playful, direct manner—almost as much as I was by his body.

"What's your name?" He cocked his head and grinned.

"Oh, sorry, I'm still not quite awake. David—nice to meet you, Mick."

He hooked a thumb in the waistband of his low-rise swimsuit and deftly pulled it off in one movement. He spread his towel over the rock and lay on his stomach and turned his head toward me. "This place is so deserted, it's hard to believe it's public. You come here a lot?"

"Not anymore. I haven't been out here in years, but my buddy and I used to come a lot during college. How 'bout you?"

"It's my first time. I just moved here from San Diego a couple of weeks ago. I don't know Austin very well yet."

"Well, you sure found this place pretty quick." I smiled at him, becoming more comfortable.

"This guy I work with told me about it."

"Where do you work?"

"At the Driskill, as a room service waiter. I'm sort of thinking about going back to school, but I don't really know what the fuck I want to do. You know what I mean?" He ran his fingers through his short wavy brown hair. "You know, when you're from California, you can't really head west, so I came east. This is as far as I got."

"It's a good place to figure out what you want to do."

"What do you do?"

"I'm a gardener."

"Cool. What do you want to do?"

"What I'm doing, being a gardener."

"Sounds like you got it made then." Mick looked from side to side along the desolate shore. "This place ever get very cruisy?"

"A friend of mine says it can be, but I only came here to swim and get some sun." I got fully hard, my erection hidden between my stomach and the towel-covered rock.

"And be naked." He smiled at me, glancing toward my bare bottom.

"Yeah, it feels nice, doesn't it? I've always worn a suit before."

"No doubt, but you got to watch your 'nads, man. That skin's delicate down there."

"I hadn't been asleep long. I think everything's going to be okay—down there." I smiled.

"You got to be careful with the sun, man. Especially on your face, you know—lines, wrinkles, even skin cancer. You got to watch that shit. Use a high SPF sunscreen and you'll do fine."

I laughed. "You sound like my friend Lexy. She's so afraid of the sun, she'll never come out here anymore."

"That's a bit extreme."

"*She's* a bit extreme."

After a while I turned away from Mick, and sat up and quickly reached for my shorts, keeping my fading erection hidden under my bent legs. I pulled on my shorts and stood on the rock.

"You taking off?"

"Yeah, I've got to get home. It was nice meeting you, Mick. Maybe I'll see you out here again sometime." I smiled. "I'll be the one with the number thirty sunscreen."

"Yeah, Dave, cool. Nice to meet you too, guy. See you 'round, maybe at the bars."

I pulled out a new t-shirt from my backpack and stripped it over my head. Mrs. Moody had given it to me. It was white with a large bunch of bright red radishes in the middle, with their leafy ends reaching in green curls above and black lettering underneath.

"See ya." I waved and began to turn.

"Cool shirt. What's it say? I can't read it. Don't have my contacts in." He pointed to his eyes.

I felt silly reading the words out loud. I looked down, seeing the words upside down. "Weed it and reap."

Mick cocked his head and smiled. "Cool."

I walked up to the nearest trail and followed it to the rest room. While standing at the urinal I read the wall. Among the usual graffiti one scrawl read, "Hippie Hollow sucks," in black marker, followed by, "It's no Poplar Avenue," in blue. I remembered Michael telling me about the strip off South Lamar, which became a cruisy area for gay men after dark. He said he checked it out once, after moving back from Houston, but that it was mostly older men.

I met Mick coming into the rest room as I was walking out.

"Hey Dave, I thought you left."

"I did. I mean, I am leaving. Had to pee."

"Yeah, me too. Hey, you in a hurry?"

"Yeah, sort of," I lied. "I'll see you, bye." I walked quickly back to the Jeep, my heart racing.

After leaving Hippie Hollow I drove around Austin for several hours, remembering the uninhibited feeling of swimming naked in the cool lake. It had been dark out for over an hour when I pulled into my driveway. I walked through the side gate and into the backyard. Abby ran up to me, collar tags clinking, and jumped up so I would pet her.

"Hey, Ab. Sorry to be gone so long." I sat on the edge of the patio. The only light came from the nearly full moon. Abby brought me a chewed-on stick and I threw it into the far corner of the yard. She brought it back and dropped it on the lawn near my feet.

"Good girl. Now go chew it up. It's okay. I don't want to play anymore." She lay down, gripped the stick between her paws, and began to chew. There was no trace of breeze, and I thought how silent Michael's sculpture would always be at this time of year. The rhythmic sound of cicadas pulsed through the cool nighttime air, helping me settle into the stillness of meditation. I tried to let go of each thought as it occurred, straining to keep my mind empty, but I wasn't able to continue for very long without one of them taking hold. I closed my eyes, breathed in the smell of a neighbor's freshly mown lawn, and stood up, stretching.

"You want to go for a ride, Abby? Come on, let's go to the car." She jumped up, dropping her stick, and ran ahead of me through the open gate. She sat on her haunches alongside the Jeep, looking back at me and wagging her tail.

I drove as I had before, aimlessly, but over the course of the next hour I found myself heading down South Lamar, eventually ending up on Poplar Avenue. It was one block west, parallel to the strip of Lamar that was home to an art film cinema, a coffeehouse, and an adult book store.

I drove down Poplar along the block that Michael had told me about, but instead of parking along its curb—like the drivers of the other two cars had done—I turned left at the first intersection. I drove up the slight hill and pulled alongside a vacant lot, underneath an old pecan tree. I was away from the streetlight that illuminated the two cars. The top was on the Jeep but the windows were unzipped. Abby sat in the small rear seat and looked onto the dark street, her snout wriggling as she took in new smells.

After about fifteen minutes two more cars and a truck pulled onto Poplar and parked. As if choreographed, the men in the first two cars got out and started walking on opposite sidewalks toward where the other cars had parked. I watched as they leaned in the cars' open windows. The man in the truck got out and began walking up the sidewalk, past the cars. When he reached the corner and turned, my breathing quickened and Abby's tail started wagging.

The man had short brown hair, combed neatly to the side, and was wearing jeans and a white polo shirt. He looked as if he were in his early forties. As he walked toward us, Abby stretched her head farther out the window in his direction. He walked right up to her. "Hi there." He began to pet her around the head and neck. "What's your name?" He looked into her eyes.

"Tell him your name, Abby?" I smiled at him.

"Hello Abby, you're pretty cute." He glanced at me. "And, so is your master." He kept petting Abby while stepping up to my window. "What's going on, guy?"

"Not much." I hadn't expected to talk with anyone.

"What're you doing parked way up here?"

"I was just out for a drive with Abby and thought it was a nice spot to park for a while." I looked down for a moment.

"Yeah, it is, isn't it? I'm Richard. How are you doing?"

"Good, and you?"

"No complaints." The man shifted his weight from side to side, his cowboy boots scraping the gravelly pavement. Abby pulled her head back a little, and panted lightly. "So I take it you're not really looking to meet anyone tonight?" He gripped the Jeep's roll bar and leaned in toward me, and I could smell a bay leaf scented cologne.

"I don't think so, not in the way you mean. I'm sorry."

"That's okay." He pushed himself back away from me. "I guess you *are* parked off the strip. Sorry to bother you, man."

"Not at all, I'm glad you came over." I didn't want him to leave. "I, I think you're pretty cute too, it's just that . . . ." I heard a car in the distance, and over his shoulder I saw it stop along Poplar.

"I hear you, man. It's okay. I just don't have all night to talk, you know what I mean? Otherwise I'd say we could go have a cup of coffee someplace." He glanced down at his boots.

"But, see, it's like I need to be home by nine, to read my son a bedtime story."

"I shouldn't have parked here."

"No, it's okay. You'll come back when you're ready."

"I guess so." I looked down again. "It was nice talking with you."

"You, too." He reached out his hand to me. "I didn't get your name."

I hesitated before looking up at him but finally looked into his face. "It's David." We shook hands.

"Well, David, you have a good night. You too, Abby." He patted her on the head and walked away, back toward the cars.

When Abby and I got home my phone machine blinked a red number one. When I pushed the button, Lexy's voice said, "Hey David. I had to work late and wanted to see if you wanted to meet for dinner somewhere. I guess not. Oh, and get a new message, please—you sound like hell. Are you okay? Give me a call later tonight or at work tomorrow."

Abby remained standing at my side, as if she were afraid of her own home. "It's okay, Ab. We're safe now." I ruffled her neck and ears and ran my fingers through her thick, soft coat. She followed me into the living room. I slouched onto the beige tweed sofa and patted my hand on the cushions for her to join me. She lay beside me and rested her head on my leg and was soon asleep. I was tired as well, but I didn't close my eyes, content to watch her sleep and let my day wash through my mind.

After a while I ran my hand from Abby's head down her back, gently waking her. She sat up, and then dropped her two front legs to the floor, stretching her long retriever's body before her back legs followed. She padded into the kitchen, then back to me, and sat on her haunches and started speaking to me, first just mouth movements without sounds, and then a few muffled barks.

"What do you want, Ab? What do you want? What?" I stared at her with my eyebrows raised, moving my head from side to side. She walked to the kitchen and I followed her and she stood in front of her empty dish. "You want some Abby chow, huh?" I filled her bowl from the bag sitting on the floor near the pantry, then grabbed a beer from the fridge and left the room to the sound of crunching, interspersed with the sound of her stirring the dry chunks around in the bowl to get at the chewy ones.

I looked through my CDs and put on an old Neil Young album, pressed repeat, and climbed back onto the couch. I went through the mail that had accumulated in my mailbox over the past week. There were several catalogs, the usual junk mail, a few bills, and a postcard from a guy I had worked with at the ad agency: "Hey Dave—The weather is here, wish you were beautiful. No kidding, Jamaica is incredible. Scored some potent ganja (sp?) from this local chick and then she . . . . A great story here, details later. Later, Maaaan. –Bill."

I tossed Bill's waterfall postcard onto the coffee table and flipped through the Land's End and Eddie Bauer catalogs. Neither the clothes nor the models could hold my interest for very long, so I set the catalogs back on top of the stack of stuff from Aunt Ivy's attorney, which had been sitting in the same spot since I first met with him.

I heard Abby lapping her water and then she appeared in the kitchen doorway, her darkened snout dripping water onto the floor. She opened her mouth and started wagging her tail before again joining me on the sofa.

I hadn't known what I should do with the legal papers—I didn't even want to look through them—so I'd simply let them sit. But I had become tired of hiding them underneath my mail. I gathered the papers and set them in my lap, shuffling past the safe-deposit box inventory and the investment portfolios to the envelope Goetz had said belonged to Uncle August. The string which closed the flap broke when I tried to unwind it. Inside was a smaller, yellowed envelope with Aunt Ivy's name typed on it and a paper-clipped note instructing Goetz's father to give the envelope to Aunt Ivy "upon the death and burial of August Schumann." The envelope was sealed. I hesitated, wondering why the older attorney had neglected to give the note to Aunt Ivy back in 1956 when Uncle August died. I sliced open the fragile crease of the envelope with my finger and unfolded the single sheet inside.

Dec. 31, 1949

My Dearest Ivy,

How do I begin such a letter? One never has practice in such things. I'm full of holiday drink, without which I would not have the strength to write this letter that I've wanted to prepare for so long now. What I want to tell you will be so very hard for you to accept and for you to believe. I am too much the coward to talk to you directly or to give this letter to you now, so I've instructed Heinrich Goetz to pass it on to you after my death. There is no expiation for me in writing, but I am moved by a selfish hope of ridding the pain from my heart. I so want to bring things to an end, at this end of such a tumultuous decade for our world, so that you may grieve appropriately and begin a new life after I'm gone.

You have certainly been an exemplary wife to me, Dear Ivy, in spite of what I have done. I know I never thanked you enough for making such a good home for me. Even now, as I am writing here in my study, I can hear you washing the dinner dishes and humming a Chopin melody.

For more than twenty-five years I know you have been fulfilling your obligation to me as a wife out of duty rather than love. I had no choice but to accept this change after what had happened, after Karl's death and the guilt you know that I must have suffered. It was much worse than you ever could have known.

I try to remember, back before the War and before the Depression, when there was such promise to our young lives. I remember how you were mad about playing ragtime and reading Fitzgerald and I was simply mad about America. Oh Ivy, I still have such joyful memories, like when I was conducting the Symphony in its early days and you were giving piano lessons to the neighborhood children after school. I loved you so much, Ivy Mae. Remember how we had dreamed of becoming rich and famous? I so wanted to tour the country with you by me side.

All the important people in the city wanted us at their parties, and they all loved you so. You were so beautiful and gracious. I don't even remember how things began to change, but after those first two years, you began visiting Clara more often and for longer periods. I know you didn't take to the city easily, but I came to imagine another reason for your visits. After I finally expressed my jealousy over your fondness for Otto, you agreed to quit visiting Clara. I knew there was no basis for my accusations of any infidelity with Otto. I had been so blinded by jealousy because of how you often commented that you envied Clara's simple life on that farm. I was envious of a common farmer and I could not stop the thoughts from coming.

After Karl was born, he reminded me of Otto. It was not that I doubted the baby's paternity, but I saw him taking you away from me, as I felt Otto had done. I tried to love him. Oh Ivy, I very much tried, but it didn't come natural to me, as it should for a father, so I began spending even more time with Symphony affairs and that first music store on Broadway. I even encouraged you to resume visiting Clara and Otto, taking the baby with you. I thought I had lost you forever.

My Dear Ivy, oh my Dear Ivy, it *was* an accident, at first. I certainly had no plan. I truly believed that he would swim. Indeed, after diving into Otto's pond that spring day so many years ago, I was overtaken with relief when I immediately located the boy. You must believe this. But as I grasped his arms, my relief turned to evil at the thought of such an effortless solution. It was less than an instant I know, but it was one of madness. Instead of saving him I pushed him deeper. I almost drowned myself before I had lodged his body under a rock at the bottom of that pond. By the time I reached the surface, I already could not believe what I had just done.

Oh, Ivy. I shall never know how I was capable of such an unspeakable act. But, oh Ivy, I was out of my mind. I thought that it would be a second chance at the life we wanted. At first I felt free, free of the thing that took my Dear Ivy away from me. It was not until later that I realized that you had also died along with Karl that April. From then on, I tried to be a decent husband to you but I knew it was too late. You were gone. Oh Ivy, I never stopped loving you. Oh Ivy, I so want to die.

August

Abby had moved away from me while I was reading the letter. She lay draped over the ottoman, chewing the fuzz off a faded tennis ball she held between her paws. I switched on the brighter lamp on the other side of the sofa, and the room's shadows became more sharply defined against the white walls. I curled up behind Abby on the couch, trying to get warm. I just sat there, feeling numb like I had when I found out Aunt Ivy had died. I began to cry as I imagined her living with Uncle August for all those years after what he had done, not knowing the truth, mourning her only child. I started to shake when I visualized Aunt Ivy's burial, the lowering of her coffin into the open grave next to Uncle August's in the late spring drizzle. She wouldn't have wanted her body there, I kept thinking, if she had ever received the letter. I threw my head against the back of the couch and clenched the cushion edges below. Abby snapped her head around, and her ears became rigid. My breathing slowed as I leaned forward and petted her. "It's okay, baby. Everything's going to be okay."

I glanced toward the letter I had dropped on the coffee table but remained sitting with Abby, listening to Neil Young rasp "Old Man" on the CD player for the third time. I felt so alone. I wanted to call Michael. I wanted someone to make me feel better. But I couldn't even make myself get off of the couch. I looked around my living room at all the things I'd collected during the years, not valuing anything in particular and then spied the toy space capsule on the top shelf before covering a yawn with my hand. I petted Abby with the toes of my cold feet before standing and looking around quickly, agitated.

I walked over to the bookshelves, grabbed the space capsule off the shelf, and with both hands flung it into the far wall as hard as I could. Pieces of plaster fell to the floor along with chunks of gray plastic. Abby's head jerked up at the noise, knocking the tennis ball she had been chewing onto the floor. It rolled to a stop in front of her on the rug. She watched me as I looked toward the rubble on the floor, seeing G.I. Joe reaching his handless arm through the space capsule's broken Plexiglas window.

When I turned to meet Abby's gaze, I felt the cool wet of tears sliding down my face. She lowered her head, centering her snout between her parallel paws, and stared at the grungy yellow ball, as if willing it to reverse itself back up to her. Her puzzled look, the tilting eyebrows and tented ears, made her seem still a puppy, all anxious to figure out her world but yet to receive enough clues.

9

"**M**r. **Goetz, Mr. Thorpe is here to see you.** Should I send him in?" Goetz's secretary looked over at me sitting on the sofa in the reception area and smiled. "Of course, I'll tell him." She replaced the phone receiver. "He'll be right out."

"Thanks." I picked up a Time magazine from the table in front of me.

With a slightly upturned smile Goetz emerged through a hall passageway and walked over to me as I stood. "David, I was planning to call you later this morning." We shook hands. "You didn't have to drive all this way." He lowered his voice as if he didn't want his secretary to hear. "Come into my office so we can talk privately."

We walked into his office. He sat behind his desk and I sat in one of the two chairs across from him. "The news isn't the best, David." He folded his hands, resting his arms on his desk as he leaned forward.

"Just tell me what you've found."

"After our phone call last week I discussed the situation with Barry and one of his PIs, Derrick Moore. They looked into your father's prison records and found nothing out of the ordinary. As you already know, he served almost all his sentence, so his supervised parole period was less than usual."

Goetz began doodling on a yellow legal pad as he spoke. "In fact, Barry spoke with the parole officer and found that after meeting with your dad for six months, the officer recommended to the court that he be released from further supervision. There were no objections." He set the pen on the pad in a gesture of finality.

"So where is he?" I leaned forward toward his desk.

"We don't know." Goetz again folded his hands. "But I have confidence we'll find out. According to the State of Texas, he's a free man, so there haven't been any substantial records after the parole officer signed off the case. But Derrick did find out that he rented an apartment in Taylor after he got out of the halfway house, and that he was able to get a job at a local grocery store. But after only a few weeks the owner found out he was an ex-con and fired him."

"So where'd he go then?"

"He hasn't been heard from since. Well, we really don't know that. It's just that Derrick's computer checks against his name and social security number haven't turned up anything, which most likely means that he's going by a different name."

"So where do you go from here?"

"I've had Barry officially put Derrick on the case. He's in Taylor now with a photo of your father. He's trying to locate people who may have known him. It's basic legwork, David. Don't worry, we'll find him. It's just going to take longer than we thought."

"I guess there's no big hurry." I leaned back in the chair. "You'll keep me updated with any information you find?"

"Absolutely. I'll call as soon as I find out anything. I realize waiting must be difficult." Goetz looked at his watch, loosened his tie and unbuttoned his collar. "But I do have some more encouraging news involving your more recent request. In fact, I don't foresee any difficulties at all. After all, you were the sole heir to your aunt's estate, and you do have just cause, so it will just be a matter of formality for me to get a court order to exhume Mrs. Schumann's body."

"Well, that's a relief."

"But are you sure you want to do this? I'm not an overly religious man, but you do realize that you're only talking about a body? It's not your aunt."

"Listen, Friedreich." I took a deep breath, trying to contain my anger. "If it weren't for your father's incompetence, my aunt would've received that letter, and she would never have consented to be buried next to the man who murdered her son."

"Okay, okay. There's no need to raise our voices. I know my firm erred and I apologize for that. I don't know how it happened. I think Dad must've practiced longer than he should have. He may have been getting senile. Hell, I don't know. Anyway, I feel horrible about his negligence. I promise I'll get everything set up for you, gratis, to try to make up for the firm's error."

"I appreciate it."

"Do you want me to arrange for another plot at Sunset Memorial?"

"No. I have something else in mind." I thought about the transcendent wildflower meadow, getting lost momentarily. "Once you have everything squared away, give me the name of the cemetery superintendent, or whoever I need to deal with, and I'll take it from there."

"Look, David, it's almost noon. Why don't you allow me to buy you lunch?" Goetz stood, unbuttoned his cuffs and rolled his sleeves halfway up his forearms. "It's not too hot out today. How about somewhere on the River Walk, say La Mansión?"

* * *

"I can't believe you're actually going through with this. You couldn't pay me enough money to go down there." Michael sat crouched in the uneven shade of the old mesquite tree near the edge of the pond, drinking Budweiser from a can. He was wearing a faded baseball cap, loose fitting khaki shorts and a white t-shirt.

"I know it seems weird, but when you think about it, it's only water." I looked out over the green surface of the pond as I sat near the end of the dock wearing a blue bathing suit, fitting rubber swim fins onto my feet.

"If the bottom is anything like the muddy goop up here at the edge, you're not going to be able to find anything. Besides, you don't even know if he would've been wearing it. Aren't things like that only ceremonial?" Michael drank from his beer. "I mean, I know I had a baptismal bracelet, and I know my mom must've saved it, but I don't think they ever made me wear it again after that day."

There he goes with that logic again, I thought, but I knew he was right. "I don't expect to find anything, I just want to do it—"

"Because it's creepy, that's why. I think you like creepy things more than me. I mean, at the least, I'd be afraid of water snakes or something."

"I don't think there're any moccasins in here, but if there are, they like to stay near the surface."

"Eeeee—David, yuck. It gives me the heebie-jeebies just thinking about the snakes alone, not to mention what else may be down there."

"Well, it's a good thing you're sitting high and dry way over there then, huh?" I smiled at Michael and picked up the yellow underwater flashlight I'd recently bought at REI. I blinked it into his partially shaded face.

Michael lifted his beer can in front of his face to block the light and eyed me around the can. "Bon voyage, frog boy!"

I turned away from him and consciously swallowed and closed my eyes tight as I fitted the diving mask over my face and scooted to the edge of the dock, before dropping into the warm water with a small splash.

I took in a deep breath before going under the surface. I could see my hands in front of me through the murky water with the help of the sunlight, but as I swam four or five feet deeper, the sunlight no longer penetrated and I turned on the flashlight, which showed a beam though the suspended particles of algae and dirt. I found the downward slope of the pond and followed it, navigating through spongy cords of lily pad stems, to the bottom.

The pressure built in my ears and I heard the piercing tone of underwater silence. At the deepest part near the center of the pond, the pressure caused my ears to ache. The light's beam showed the water much clearer than near the surface but still with a greenish hue. As I directed the light to the center of the pond I could see several large rocks lodged into the bottom, similar to those along the creek.

I hurriedly swam over and glanced around the edges of the rocks, before pushing myself toward the surface as the pangs of running out of air became urgent.

Michael had taken off his t-shirt and had moved to the dock where he was watching the surface of the pond. "What'd you find?"

"Just some big rocks near the center." I was breathing hard. "It's a little deeper than I thought though, probably about twelve feet at the deepest."

"No snakes?"

"Not even a fish."

"They're probably scared as hell with you down there."

"Probably." I inhaled as completely as I could and again went under. This time I swam straight for the deepest part, following the narrow, conical passageway created by my flashlight. I swam to the grouping of rocks, my heart beginning to beat faster. I ran my hand across one of them and silt swirled around to cloud my view, so I swam to another, careful not to stir up anymore dirt. I moved around the rock and flinched when I inadvertently disturbed a large catfish, which had been hiding near the edge of the rock. Its tail fin swooshed more silt, obscuring my vision near an outcropping from the rock.

I ran my fingers along the exposed mud and gravel bottom as the light's beam traced my movements. When the water cleared I directed the light under the rock and my gut contracted, as I suddenly realized it was the spot where Karl must have died, and where his small body decomposed decades before. I crouched near the rock, holding on to the outcropping and squeezed my eyes shut as I used up the rest of my air in small, clenching exhalations.

I pushed myself to the surface and didn't even look toward Michael as I took in a large amount of air and went back under. I kneeled at the same rock, remaining steady by holding onto the rock. Again I fanned at the bottom with my hand, directing the light in front of me, and waited for the silt to settle. The pebbly sand and mud floor of the pond was all that I saw until I pushed myself back and looked beneath the rock. I saw a little mud-filled bowl about the size of my hand. I moved the light around and saw two more bone fragments about a foot and a half away from the skull cap. The light beam shined on the skull as I picked it up and held it in front of me. I rested it on the crown of my head for moment, turned off the light, and then clutched the curved bone against my chest as I curled up into a ball and sank to the bottom.

I again surfaced without talking to Michael and returned to the same spot near the rock, not ready to leave the connection I had for so long wanted to find. I put the bone fragments into the small mesh bag I had tucked into my bathing suit. I directed the light around the rocks as I breathed out air bubbles through my nose. Just as I was about to resurface the flashlight caught a small gleam among the sand and mud. I reached to grab at it, expecting and hoping it was Karl's baptismal bracelet, but it was a partially buried coin. I rubbed at its surface and saw that it was gold. I passed the light one last time over the area surrounding the outcropping and propelled myself upward, as I tucked the coin into the pocket inside the waistband of my bathing suit.

I broke the surface, more out of breath than the previous times. I heard Michael as I swam toward the dock with the mesh bag dragging alongside, its drawstring hanging from my forearm.

"What's going on? I was starting to get worried about you." He was sitting at the end of the dock when I looked up at him. It felt good to see him there waiting for me, concerned.

"I'm okay. I think I've had enough. Help me get out of here. I set all my things on the dock, careful to hide the mesh bag under the mask and flippers as Michael turned to toss his empty beer can on the shore near our packs. He grabbed my hands, and as he started pulling me out, the board on which he was standing began to crack. I let go of him as he fell forward and I went underwater so he wouldn't fall on top of me. When I surfaced we were both laughing. We swam toward the shore near a muddy clearing pocked with cow tracks, the only edge that wasn't thick with reeds and cattails. Our feet sank deep into the mud as we tried to get out. While we were trudging out of the last foot of water Michael fell forward, covering himself with mud.

"Shit, David. Help me out of this crap." He rolled over and sat in the gluey goop and wiped at his face, smearing the mud away from his eyes.

I started to laugh. "You look pretty stupid." I grabbed his hands and as I tried to yank him up, he pulled me into the mud next to him. We both started laughing and, like ten-year-olds at a sleepover, found it difficult to stop. After several minutes of just sitting there, finding alternative angles by which to be amused by our situation, we helped each other up and trudged through the muck until it became firmer, and then drier, ground. We walked over to our packs and sneakers near the trunk of the mesquite.

"Jesus, David, look at us." Michael was covered with even more mud than me. His teeth gleamed against his slick brown face.

"I feel so much better." I started laughing again. "You wouldn't believe." You would not believe, I thought.

"Being covered in slimy, cow-slobber mud makes you feel good?" Michael looked at me, incredulous.

"I guess so. Lexy would be so proud, it's like a full-body mask."

"Yeah, yeah. Well, I'm not waiting for this one to dry. It'd wring me to death. I'm going to wash off." Michael started to walk toward the dock.

I glanced toward the dock and saw my snorkeling gear sitting near the board that broke. "I don't think that's such a good idea. I think the whole thing's about to go. We can clean up down at the creek. I just need to get my stuff first."

I carefully walked on the last good boards of the dock and retrieved my gear. When I returned to the tree Michael was stuffing his socks and t-shirt into his pack. I did the same with my things.

Michael started to walk away from the tree, his pack hanging from a bare shoulder, which was caked with mud. "So you didn't find the mysterious bracelet, did you Nancy Drew? Or are you a Hardy Boy?"

"Har, har. Hardly. No, I didn't find it. As usual, you were right. "But," I reached into the pocket of my muddy bathing suit, "I did find this." I held the coin in front of his face, which was framed by wavy blond hair frosted with brown mud.

"That's gold!" He took the coin from my hand. "What kind is it? Were there more?"

I took back the coin and rubbed at the dirt on its surface with my thumb. "It's a twenty dollar gold piece, see?" I held its face toward him. There were lots of them in Aunt Ivy's safety deposit box at the bank. The woman at Alamo National said they're worth about three-hundred bucks a piece now." I looked at the coin again and its date read 1925. I was suddenly startled to see it in my hand, and I threw it back into the pond almost by reflex.

"What'd you do that for?"

"Whoever put it there wanted it there. I doubt it merely fell out of anyone's bathing suit." I stared at the surface of the pond. "Come on, let's get cleaned up."

"You're really weird sometimes, Thorpe." He clapped his hand on my shoulder as we continued walking toward the creek. "But Lexy's right, you're cute when you're weird."

Michael pulled a joint and a lighter out of his pack as I took off my shoes and dipped them into the flowing water to wash away the dried mud.

"You want any?" Michael offered the joint to me and I took it and the lighter from him. I lit up, inhaled and gave it back to him. We passed it back and forth while we sat on a large rock in the shade of a willow tree, dangling our feet into the bubbly water that flowed between two rocks.

"Guess what." Michael took a drag from the joint and held it, pursing his lips.

"What?"

He exhaled. "I finished Copper One."

"Really? When?"

"Just yesterday. It was sort of anticlimactic, though."

"How so?" I finished the joint, snubbed out the roach and set it by Michael's pack.

"Well, it's sort of like you can't fully experience it unless you can see it *and* hear it—and it's not too windy in my studio, you know." He laughed.

"But you have heard it, right?" I noticed that the mud had almost completely dried on our skin, forming an ashen layer which was beginning to flake off. Michael's shorts and my bathing suit were still covered with mud. A breeze penetrated the thick woods into the creek valley, rustling the willow leaves around us.

"Oh yeah, I've heard it. The guy who helped me tune it was great. He brought along this huge fan to simulate different wind speeds. It was really cool." Michael lay back on the rock, his torso now lit by the sun.

I lifted my feet out of the water and turned toward Michael. "And you're happy with how it turned out?"

"Yeah, I guess I am. But you know, I've got mixed feelings about it. Now that it's done, I'm not in the process of creating it anymore. It's almost like I wish I was still working on it."

"I think that's natural. You just need to start thinking about your next piece."

"Yeah." He sighed. "Geez, it's hot out today." He stretched his body across the rock, his stomach muscles flexing into gentle ridges, and yawned.

"Yeah, the water will feel good."

"I'm almost ready." Michael sat up and looked at me. "How do you feel?"

"Good. And high, of course." I laughed. "But I am glad I swam in the pond, though I don't really want to talk about it now. Some other time, okay?"

"Sure. Whatever you want is fine. I'm sure it was pretty rough, being down there where . . . ."

"Yeah." I hopped off the rock into the thigh-deep water that formed a pool below the small waterfall. I almost lost my balance, but Michael caught me by the arm.

"You okay?"

"Yeah, the bottom is a little uneven. Be careful."

"Thanks. I'm not quite ready to come in. I'm sort of in that stoner-immobile mode."

I crouched and began to wash my arms and legs. "You know, there's even mud inside my bathing suit. I'm going to have to rinse it out."

"Yeah, my shorts too." He rocked from side to side, watching me wash my chest and shoulders. "It's pretty squishy down there. I'll be in in a minute . . . but David?"

"What?" I untied the string to my bathing suit.

Michael sat there, leaning back on the rock, the sun lighting the blond hairs on his lower abdomen.

"What?" I repeated.

"Well, just don't weird out if I get a hard-on. You know, I am gay after all," he smiled, "and there's just something about being naked around a good-looking guy." He laughed. "I don't know what it is, but . . . ." Michael dropped his glance into his lap.

"That's okay." I pulled off my swimsuit, revealing my growing erection. "It doesn't look like you'll be alone." I walked deeper into the pool and began washing the suit in front of me.

Michael jerked his head toward mine, and I almost started to laugh, thinking about what was going through his head. But he only smiled, as if he were playing along into some long preplanned fantasy. He took off his cap, ran his fingers through his hair, and stepped into the water. "It's warmer than it looks." He smiled again as he unbuttoned his shorts and pulled them off along with his muddy underwear.

I wrung out my bathing suit and tossed it on the rock and walked up to Michael, who had crouched in the pool and was rinsing out his shorts. He looked up at me standing over him, and then stood up and tossed his shorts and underwear up onto the rock.

He looked down between us. "You were right. I guess we have something in common here."

I smiled and reached my arm out toward him and touched my fingers just below his chest and held them there for a moment before looking up into his eyes and then running my fingertips down his stomach, over the dried mud which had reconstituted into a broad smear. I ran my hands up along his sides and then held his head in my hands and pulled his face into mine and we kissed. He wrapped his arms around me and we kneeled into the warm, flowing water.

* * *

"I'm Elaine Jacoby." The older woman reached out a slender hand toward me. "You must be Helen's gardener?"

I shook her hand. "Yes, David Thorpe. Nice to meet you." I was standing near the punch bowl along the spread of food Mrs. Moody had had catered for her birthday bridge party.

"You do such creative things with Helen's yards," she gushed. "Do you think I could convince you to take on mine?" Mrs. Jacoby speared a piece of watermelon from her buffet plate.

"Actually, I only work for Helen these days. See, I don't do it for the money anymore because . . . ."

"David, I didn't know you were here." Mrs. Moody walked over to where Mrs. Jacoby and I were talking.

"I've only been here a few minutes. I didn't see you when I came in."

"I've been in the kitchen finishing up things with the caterer."

"Well, let me give the birthday girl a hug." I hugged Mrs. Moody and kissed her on the cheek. "Happy birthday, Helen.

You look beautiful." She wore an ivory-colored linen dress on which was pinned a lavender-tinted orchid.

"So do you, David. I've never seen you so, so . . . ."

"Clean? I just got back from the farm and showered." I was wearing navy blue shorts and a white button-down shirt cuffed at the sleeves.

"No, that's not all. It's your face, your smile, it's everything. Look Elaine, look at his eyes. He looks radiant, don't you think?"

"Oh Helen, stop. You're embarrassing the boy. Look, he's blushing."

"Oh don't stop, Helen, go on." I grinned at them, and we all laughed.

"I don't know what you did today, but whatever it was, keep doing it."

"Oh, I plan on it." I laughed.

"I like the sound of that laugh." Mrs. Moody poured herself a cup of punch. "Would you like some, David?"

"Yes, thanks." I held a cup over the bowl and Mrs. Moody ladled the cloudy red mixture, filling my cup to the brim.

"Elaine, would you like a refill?"

Mrs. Jacoby moved her empty plate over her cup. "No thank-you, Helen. I think I'm going to have some coffee instead. I've got to keep my wits for bridge." Mrs. Jacoby turned to me. "It was nice meeting you, David." She turned to Mrs. Moody. "You're so lucky to have him, Helen. Really, he's an absolute doll." Mrs. Jacoby walked into her living room where the other women were gathering near the three card tables.

"Elaine is too much sometimes, don't you think?" Mrs. Moody sipped her punch.

"She seems like a nice lady."

"Did you bring a friend?" Mrs. Moody looked around the room.

"Yes, I brought my buddy Michael."

"How nice, I can't wait to meet him. Where is he?"

"He's having a problem with a contact lens. He's in the bathroom." I looked toward the hallway. "There he is."

126

Michael walked up to where we were standing, smiling. He was wearing a pair of my khaki shorts and my blue chambray shirt, cuffed at his forearms and untucked.

"Hey Michael, this is Mrs. Moody. Mrs. Moody, Michael."

"Nice to meet you, Michael." Mrs. Moody reached out her hand.

"Not *the* Mrs. Moody, supreme philanthropist and benefactor extraordinaire?" Michael stood up straighter and his smile widened.

"Of course not," Mrs. Moody laughed. "I would have to be one hundred and fifty years old, at least. Suddenly seventy-five doesn't seem so bad." We all laughed and Michael turned red. "You're referring to my late husband's grandmother. She and her husband were quite the philanthropists. Unfortunately, I can't match that grandeur."

"Sorry for the *faux pas*." Michael looked around the room. "You have a lovely home. I've been admiring your paintings."

"All the credit must go to my late husband, Dr. Randolph Moody. He was the collector." She finished her punch and dropped her cup into the wicker waste basket at the end of the table.

"Everything is well put together here, very contemporary and minimal. It's certainly no little-old-lady house, that's for sure."

"Oh Michael, you have no idea how you have just made my day." She reached over and gave him a hug. "Well, boys. Eat and drink all you want. I've got to visit with my other guests. It was nice meeting you Michael. You and David are always welcome here."

"Yeah, but where was he when I was sweating like a pig, digging that trench out back?" I said, smiling at Mrs. Moody.

Michael held up his hands out in front of his face. "These are the hands of an *artiste*. I certainly can't denigrate them with manual labor."

We all laughed and Mrs. Moody threw one hand up in the air as she turned and walked away.

"Good show. You've won her over."

"You think?" He again held up his hands. "These are the hands of an *artiste*—"he lowered his voice, "and I want to put them down your pants."

I laughed and pushed his arms back down to his side. "Maybe later." Our eyes met and we grinned and then looked away.

"Really, David, she's a hoot. I love her."

Michael looked through the French doors out past the patio. "I didn't know she had a swimming pool. You think I could be her pool boy?"

"Here, have some punch." I ladled a cup full and handed it to him. "It's actually pretty good. It tastes spiked—vodka or something."

Michael sipped from the cup. "Definitely vodka." He wriggled his nose and took a large drink. "How many of these have you had?"

I refilled my glass. "This will be three, I think."

"Well, let's move away from here and get some food. Everyone will think you're a lush."

We filled two plates and took them outside to a patio table, just as the women were dividing into fours for bridge. We ate quickly, shedding our manners after leaving the house.

"God, this stuff is great." Michael spoke with his mouth full, pointing to the hummus sprinkled with paprika and minced parsley.

"Yeah, everything's really good. We can go back for more when we're through."

"Oh, I'm counting on it." Michael smiled, swallowed, and then took a drink of punch. He sat back in his chair, his face flattening. "I'm really happy about things, David." He raised his eyebrows. "You?"

"I'm pretty happy, too. But for more reasons than you think." I picked up my pack I'd set on the patio earlier and unzipped it.

"What's in there?" Michael continued eating, glancing at me pulling the mesh bag from the pack. "More gold coins?"

"I didn't feel like showing you earlier, but . . . ." I lifted the three bone fragments from the bag and set them on the table between us. "This was my other find today."

Michael set his fork down on his plate and wiped his mouth with the napkin that had been spread over his lap. "Are those what I think they are?"

"They're all that's left of Karl's body. I'm going to bury them on the farm next month, once it gets cooler out."

"Jesus, David, so that's what you were really looking for?"

"In a way, yeah. I wanted to find a part of him at least, but I didn't know if there would be anything left."

"What was it like down there?"

"Pretty weird. I didn't want to admit it earlier, but I really was scared to go down there."

"See, I knew it."

I smiled at Michael. "And it *was* pretty fucking scary too, I have to say." I looked toward my punch glass before picking it up and taking a drink.

"It even creeped me out to see you go down there." Michael scrunched his napkin and dropped it on his plate. "Well, anyway, I'm glad it's over with."

"Me too."

Michael raised his cup. "Here's to putting unpleasant things behind us . . . ."

"Yes." I raised mine. "And, to our fabulous future."

Our cups touched with a muted click as I moved my leg under the table and slowly rubbed it along Michael's bare calf.

10

I reached for my coffee as Lexy was refilling it for the third time with her dark chicory blend, tapping my feet on the floor in a failed attempt at a snappy cadence.

"Hold on, you're going to burn your hand." She finished pouring and set the glass server on the Mr. Coffee sitting on her cluttered kitchen counter. Sunlight streamed through the window, lighting suspended dust particles in vertical sheets above the table. "Do you want another scone or more melon?"

I looked down at my plate smeared with blackberry jam and scattered with crumbs and the orange and green tapered curls of cantaloupe rinds. "No thanks. Everything was great though." I began drumming my fingertips on her faux wood-grain table.

Lexy finished wrapping the leftover scones in plastic and joined me at the table, giving me a sideways glance. "Maybe you shouldn't have any more coffee. How many cups have you had?"

"I think it's my fourth."

Lexy put her hand over my cup. "I'm cutting you off. I haven't seen you this wired with nothing to say since the time

I broke into your apartment to surprise you with my attempt at Italian cooking and . . . ."

"Seduction?" I smiled at her, determined to seize the opening.

"I didn't have to, remember? It was you who ended up coming on to me."

"You're right. I did want you." I remembered that evening six years before, how Michael had called my office to tell me he'd decided to move to Houston the next day.

"But only for that one night. I know, David. We don't have to go through it all again." Lexy pushed her hair away from her face and held it in a short ponytail for a moment. "Well, you didn't stay wired for long that night—but I don't think two bottles of Chianti would be such a hot idea at ten o'clock on a Sunday morning."

I laughed. "I guess I'm more anxious than speedy. It's just that I've wanted to talk to you about some things this morning and here we are, finished with breakfast and all, and I've hardly said a word." I began turning my fork over and over, clinking it against the plate.

Lexy reached her hand forward and covered the noise. "Just spit it out, David. You know you can tell me anything." She looked into my eyes, her hand still covering mine.

"I'm sorry." I set the fork tine side down on my plate.

"You're not sick are you?" Her face softened.

"No, no. I'm fine. In fact I'm great." I looked down at a blackberry jam stain on the table cloth. "I guess that's the problem. I want to share this wonderful news with you, but I'm not so sure you're . . . ."

"Look, I think I know what you're going to tell me, so why put either of us through this." Lexy put her elbows on the table, folded her arms and leaned forward. "It could be only one of two things: either you're about to propose marriage to me, or you're going to tell me you're gay—and I gave up on the first one ever happening years ago."

I opened empty hands in front of me. "Sorry, no ring." I tried to laugh.

She sat up straight and pushed her hair behind her ears. "Look, David. I'm sorry that you've apparently been so nervous about talking to me about this. You know you're always going to be my friend no matter what, but I'm not going to lie to you and tell you I'm thrilled. I will be though," she took a deep breath, "just give me time." She leaned back in her chair and showed a sad, hurt smile. "I love gay men, you know that. Look at me and Michael. I guess I just never wanted to have to love you like that."

"I know, Lex. Believe me, for the longest time I didn't want this either. I've fought it for most of my life and . . . ."

"I'm sure it's been hard. And even though I felt this coming a long time ago, it's difficult for me, too. It makes me think, okay Lexy, what the fuck's wrong with you? Why do you always fall in love with unavailable men?" She gulped her coffee. "Think of my track record, David. Nick was married, Mateo lived in El Salvador, and now you've confirmed it, you're gay. What's that say about me?"

"I don't know, Lex. I don't think it has to say anything, especially not anything bad." I exhaled, becoming more comfortable with the attention focused back on Lexy's life. "Plus, it's not like we're talking about a dozen men here. I know the thing with Nick really hurt you, but like you said at the time, it was quite an adventure and helped you grow up. And Matt, well, I can still hear you rave about the sex." Lexy tried to resist a confirming smile, turning it into more of a smirk. "And, well, okay, so we never had the type of relationship that you wanted, but I'll always love you. You know that." She just sat there, looking at me as if I hadn't yet said enough. "And what about Jack? He's available, and from what I can tell, very ready and willing." I smiled.

"Yeah, Jack." Lexy rolled her eyes and they started to tear.

"What's wrong? I thought everything was okay between you two?"

"God help me, but I think I'm starting to fall in love with him." She blinked her eyes and drank from her cup. "He's just such a puppy, you know, and I don't know why, but the whole thing really scares me."

"I'm no shrink, but maybe you're feeling this way because he *is* available, and before now you weren't ready. Just dive in, Lex. He's a good guy. He's good to you, he's got a good job—and he's very cute."

"You think?"

"Oh yeah, he's quite a babe?" I smiled.

Lexy laughed. "Look at you. You've only been out, for what, all of five minutes, and you're already fantasizing about my boyfriend?"

"I am not. I'm not into straight guys anyway." I pushed my plate aside, grinning, and rested my arms on the table before looking back up at her. "Look, I'm the last one here qualified to give advice on love, and opening your heart to someone is never easy, but it's just about the best thing you can do in this world. Everything involves risk, but I think even I've finally learned that if you never make a move you never get anywhere."

"You're right." She squeezed her eyes shut, threw her head back so that it faced the ceiling, and groaned. "Oh David, why do we have to go through such shit?"

"Because it's not shit. It's wonderful. It's part of being human." I pounded my fist on the table and she looked at me. "We are so fucking lucky, Lexy. Sure, we've been through crap, but who hasn't? But look at us now. There's no more time for whining."

"God, David, you sound like a sage. Being out really agrees with you. How'd you get such insight?"

"I don't mean to tell you what to do." I lowered my voice. "Look, I didn't come over here this morning just to come out to you. I also wanted to apologize for hurting you the way I did. Feeling rejected sucks, especially when you don't know why." Now my eyes began to tear, and I wanted to hold Lexy but figured I shouldn't.

Lexy closed her eyes, forcing tears to roll down her cheeks, and began to speak. "I know now that none of it was intentional, but God, David, it did hurt. You don't realize how much you hurt me . . . ."

"I'm sorry, I . . . ."

"For so long, both during and after college, I held on to that slight possibility that you'd someday come around and want me. Even after I lost the weight I still felt repulsive because *you* weren't interested. You can't imagine how bad I felt." She sat up straighter and wiped the tears from her face. "If I would've considered the chance that you might be gay back then, maybe I would've felt different. But you dated other girls, for God's sake."

"I know, I'm sorry. What was I thinking?" I thunked the palm of my hand on my head, attempting to make Lexy laugh. "If I could have accepted the truth about myself then, I would've spared both of us a lot of grief. I'm really sorry, Lex. I never meant to hurt you."

"I guess I acted pretty ridiculous back then, trying to snare you. It does seem pretty funny now. You've always been pretty cute, David, but let's face it, you're certainly no God's gift to women." She suddenly stopped talking and we stared at each other.

"You're right," I said soberly, then cracked a smile. "I'm God's gift to men." We both started laughing.

"And you do make me laugh, especially when you're not even trying, but you know what I mean. "You're a scruffy little mutt—adorable, but you're not going to take home the blue ribbon at the show."

"Thanks a lot, Lex. I think I've had enough of your compliments." I grinned.

"Jack reminds me of you, in that way, maybe because he's just young. But, he's more . . . well, let's just say he's better groomed." She stood up, walked over to me, leaned down and gave me a hug. "I'm glad you came over this morning."

"Over *and out*." I smiled at her.

Lexy groaned and then smiled and stood up, stretching her arms overhead. "I feel like such a slug this morning. We should take a walk and get some air." She walked over to the sink, filled her coffee cup with tap water and poured it on a potted ivy, and turned to me. "So, what about Michael?" She spoke hesitantly. "I assume you've already told him?" Lexy leaned against the sink.

"I didn't have to."

"He knew, huh?"

"Well, not exactly."

"What do you mean?"

"Well, we sort of . . . ."

"You sort of what?"

"Well, it's just that, we had sex yesterday."

"Get out, are you serious?"

"Absolutely. It was incredible." I tried to contain my giddiness.

"That is so wild, David. I'm so happy for you."

"Yeah, I'm pretty wired about it."

"I don't mean to be nosey, well, of course I mean to be nosey, but, is it more than just sexual? Do have feelings for him? I know that he . . . ."

"That he what?"

"Nothing, I don't know what I was going to say. I lost my train of thought."

"You big liar. What were you going to say? You know that he what?"

"I swore never to tell, and you know how I can keep a secret."

I raised my eyebrows.

"Okay, so I haven't been that good in the past, but . . . ."

"Come on, Lexy, you're my best friend. If you're going to break a confidence, it should be for me."

"Well, okay. It's just that, well, he thought you were straight, even after I started thinking you probably weren't. But, he once told me, he wished you weren't."

"Really? When?"

"It was during a phone call soon after he had moved to Houston. He had called to apologize for leaving town without seeing me, and for leaving you to explain. But the ironic thing is that I'm now explaining to you for him."

"Huh? What are you talking about?"

"I mean the real reason he moved to Houston. You must've thought of the possibility over the years?" Lexy spoke pointedly, as if she were resisting telling me. "He moved to

Houston because of you, David. He told me he loved you, and he didn't mean just as a friend."

"Oh, wow, are you serious?" I leaned back in my chair, clasping my hands behind my head and closing my eyes briefly.

"But he was too afraid of how you would react. You know, because you were supposedly straight." Lexy raised her eyebrows and smiled. "I don't think his feelings have changed."

11

I **stood naked in front of the fogged** bathroom mirror and attempted to shave. I pushed open the bathroom door with my foot, and the steam from my shower lowered and folded around the door frame and slid out of the room. Abby lay in the hall, just out of reach of the door. I bent down and rubbed behind her ears and then returned to the mirror.

I positioned the razor on my lathered cheek and began scraping the two-day stubble from my face as the cooler air cleared the mirror. I shaved more carefully than I had in years and thought about what Lexy had said, about Michael's feelings for me. The phone rang but I let the machine get it, thinking it was only Lexy reminding me to scrub my fingernails. After the final stroke of the razor, I splashed my face with handfuls of very hot water followed my handfuls of very cold, causing my skin to flush.

I ran my fingers through my short damp hair. I hadn't worn it that short since I was a kid, but Lexy's stylist, Mara, suggested it, saying I needed a change, big time, from my typical black bird's nest of hair. I squeezed a small amount of clear gel out of a tube and rubbed it into my hair, combing and arranging the spiky hairs with my fingers in varying ways, not satisfied with any of my attempts.

I walked into my bedroom, grabbed some underwear and a pair
of black socks from my bureau and put them on, carefully arranging the seams of the socks across my toes. I noticed a breeze through the open window, blowing only slightly cool across my bed. I thought about how tired I was of the heat and how much I was ready for summer to be over for good.

I slid the new tuxedo shirt from its plastic covered hanger and held it by a finger as I stood in front of the full-length mirror attached to my bedroom door. I admired my body, which had become tanned and quite buff from a long summer of yard work and swimming, before slipping into the shirt and buttoning it. I put on the black pants and cummerbund and then attempted to tie the bowtie as the salesman at Grosdorf's had demonstrated. I slipped into the jacket, and walked around my living room looking for my wallet and keys when I remembered the phone call. I turned the volume up on my machine, pressed the answer button, and listened as Goetz's voice began.

"Hello David, it's Friedreich Goetz. Sorry to be calling you on a Saturday evening, but Barry's PI just called me. He's located your father. I would, of course, prefer to talk with you directly, because I know how important this is to you, but as I speak I'm heading out of town to attend a conference in Galveston. Here's the basic information, you might want to write this down. Your father's going by the name of D.J. Thorson, and he's closer than we thought. He's living in New Braunfels. He doesn't have a phone, but the address is 612 East Pecan Street. I'll give you a call on Tuesday when I return with more details. If you need to reach me sooner, my cell phone number is 652-8486. Hope everything works out the way you want it to."

I slipped my wallet into the inside pocket of my jacket and picked up the keys from the table next to the couch. It was hard for me to believe that my dad was only forty-five minutes away in a town I drove through every time I went to San

Antonio. I filled a glass with water, took it into the living room, and sat on the couch next to Abby. She moved closer to me and set her head on my leg. I petted her with short strokes to her head and didn't want to stop.

The phone rang and I reached to pick it up on the first ring. "Hello."

"Where the hell are you? Why aren't you here yet? Michael and I have been waiting for almost twenty minutes."

"Sorry, Lex. What time is it?" I looked at my bare wrist and wondered where I had put my watch.

"It's almost six. What's going on?"

"Nothing. I'm leaving now, bye." I hung up the phone and patted Abby goodbye. Standing to leave, I drank the remaining water from my glass, and as I walked toward the door I looked in the mirror that hung next to it and wondered if my dad would even recognize me.

* * *

"I can't believe everything fell into place—and so quickly." Michael sipped champagne from the fluted crystal glass, which he held by the stem. "Can you even believe it, fifty thousand dollars? I'm floored, but totally psyched." He was wearing a classic tux similar to mine, which he had rented. Lexy had pinned an ivory-colored rose boutonniere on his lapel and his hair had been trimmed and slicked back with pomade smelling of citrus and cloves.

"That is fantastic, but the best part is that Copper One has a home." I stood near Michael in the middle of the ballroom on the second floor of the LBJ Presidential Library. I looked around for Lexy, wondering where she had disappeared to as soon as we arrived.

"And what a home it is . . . ."

"I'll say, the grounds of the Fine Arts Library—you can't get much better than that."

"Yeah, it feels like a real coup." He grabbed two more glasses of champagne from the tray of a young, blond cater-waiter who paused in front of us, smiling knowingly at

Michael and me, before continuing with his rounds. "But it's not Copper One anymore. I changed the name last week, right before Lexy called me with the news about securing a patron."

"So, what's the new name?"

"I want it to be a surprise." Michael sipped from his glass. "You'll find out at the dedication tomorrow morning. It will only last a few minutes, but I'm still pretty psyched."

"I don't know if I can wait." I sipped from the champagne and my mouth puckered at its sour effervescence.

"You'll have to. Nobody knows except me and the engraver, and I'm not telling." Michael pointedly looked at me from head to toe. "You look pretty spiffy there, sporto. No wonder that waiter couldn't take his eyes off you." Michael smiled and raised his eyebrows as he drank from his glass.

"Yeah, right." I looked around, feigning disinterest in the compliment. "So who's the eccentric dowager this time?"

"Very funny." Michael looked at me sideways and smiled. "Lexy said it was an anonymous donor, but you're right, she is an old woman from Highland Park in Dallas, some UT alum from way back, class of '28."

"So how'd she find out about you?"

"She doesn't exactly know me or my work. It's like, well, Lexy said this woman's grandson was an artist, but that he'd been killed in a car wreck when he was pretty young."

"How tragic . . . ."

So anyway, in honor of him she's been supporting new artists ever since. Isn't that great?" Michael laughed. "Not about her grandson dying and all, of course, but that she *wants* to give money to someone like *me*."

"Too bad you can't thank her."

"Lexy said I can write a thank-you note and that a foundation staffer would forward it to her." Michael looked around at the guests, who were mainly middle-aged or older couples, grouped in fours, talking loudly and laughing. "Anyway, Lexy said these type of contributions are common, especially among the very rich." Michael unpinned his rose, smelled it, and set it on a nearby table. "She says they want to stay anonymous because they don't want to be hit up by every open hand."

"I can see that."

"I guess so, but if it were me doing the giving, I'd want the guy to know, so he could lavish me with loads and loads of gratitude."

"You would." I smiled. "Let's get some food and find Lexy."

Michael followed me as I navigated a path through the crowd filling the ballroom. Crystal chandeliers were suspended on gold filigree chains from the twelve-foot ceiling. Large floral displays accented with black-speckled yellow and red Asiatic lilies and spindly willow branches served as center pieces to the round tables throughout the room. Garlands of lily-of-the-valley and ivy lay twined among the buffet table, spread thick with platters of colorful, rich foods. Larger sprays of flowers and tall candlesticks were metered across the table, serving as a dramatic backdrop for the food.

While we were making our way through the buffet line, filling our plates, a small orchestra in the far corner of the room began to play. I looked toward the music and saw Lexy. She was walking toward us in a low-cut, sleeveless black dress that ended at mid-thigh, black pumps, and a short strand of pearls. Her hair was pinned up, with dark tendrils spilling over each ear.

"I've been looking for you guys. I should've known you'd be by the food." Lexy shifted her weight from one foot to the other. "These heels are killing me. I shouldn't have let that saleswoman talk me into a seven and a half."

"What's up, besides bad shoes?" I smiled directly into her face. "Geez, they make you tall, though."

"I'm glad you're in such a good mood." Lexy picked up a half full glass of champagne from the buffet table. "Is this yours?" She drank from the glass before I could shake my head no, so I changed it to nodding yes. "I'm in a good mood, too. Guess who just arrived downstairs?"

As we all stepped away from the buffet to let others pass, Michael turned to Lexy and waved his hands. "Hi Lexy, remember me, your star artist?"

"Of course, darling," Lexy drawled in an affected Eastern European accent, "You look fabulous, you tall, blond god, you." We all laughed and Lexy turned to me, dropping the accent. "You do too, David, I've been meaning to tell you. I love the cut." She rubbed her hand up along the back of my head. "Oooh, I love the feel of that," she said, writhing in her slinky dress.

"Thanks, Lex. Okay now, so who's the bigwig that just showed up?" I held my hand over the warm food on my plate.

"I like your hair too, David." Michael pointedly smiled at Lexy. "It makes you look really hot."

Lexy laughed. "Come on, guys. Shhhh. Listen, it's Lady Bird. Her limo just pulled up downstairs. She'll be up in a few minutes. Oh God, I need another glass of champagne." The blond waiter passed by and Lexy took two glasses off his tray. She gulped one, set the empty glass on a tray standing on a folding table, and began to sip from the other.

"Geez, Lex. What's with the drinking? Aren't you technically *at work*?"

"I've been a nervous wreck all day. You know what a bitch my boss from hell Mrs. Delgado can be, and I know she's just looking for something to go wrong tonight so she can blame me on Monday. Sometimes I wonder why I just don't quit, you know." Lexy's voice became louder. "I'm just so sick of taking shit from her. Did you know she gives me a lot of shit, David. A lot of shit, that's what that woman gives me. A lot of shit."

"Shhh, Lex. People are staring. I think you need to eat something. Here." I pushed my plate toward her, but she held up her hand and turned her head to the side.

"Ugh, I couldn't eat a thing. I don't think I could keep it down, and that's all I need tonight, to toss my cookies in front of my boss."

"Or on her." I laughed, feeling the effects of the champagne as well.

"Now, *I'd* pay to see that," Michael said.

Lexy's mouth dropped open wide and she held a hand to her face. "Come on, guys, you want to get me fired? This is the best job I've ever had."

Michael and I looked at each other, stifling our laughter. Lexy sipped from her champagne and giggled. The orchestra music became louder as it played "The Yellow Rose of Texas." People quit talking and turned, following something with their eyes.

"There they are Lexy, they're heading over here, toward you." I pointed with my chin.

"Oh my God, really? Is it really her? Is my lipstick okay?" Lexy drank the last from her glass and set it on the table.

"Yes, you look beautiful." I whispered loudly, "Turn around—now!"

Lexy turned around quickly, almost losing her balance, just as Lady Bird Johnson and several women and two tall men stopped in front of us.

"Hello, Lexy." Mrs. Delgado waved toward us. She stood next to another woman who stood next to Mrs. Johnson, who wore a tailored, cream-colored linen suit and matching pumps. "Everything seems to have turned out very nice, Lexy." She looked toward the first woman, "This is Mrs. Dunworthy, Mrs. Johnson's executive assistant." Lexy and the woman shook hands. "And it's an honor for me to introduce Lady Bird Johnson." Mrs. Delgado gestured, almost dramatically, to the former First Lady.

"It's such a pleasure to have you here Mrs. Johnson. May I call you Lady Bird?" Lexy grinned.

"Why of course, dear." Mrs. Johnson glanced at Mrs. Dunworthy and Mrs. Delgado before looking back at Lexy. "I heard you orchestrated this wonderful event, and I wanted to thank you personally." Mrs. Johnson extended her hand, on which she wore a gold ring with a large emerald, and lightly shook Lexy's hand. Her gray hair was heavily veined with white and she looked much older than I thought she would, but as her large smile lifted the wrinkled skin draped over her cheekbones, she radiated the charm of the cultivated First Lady remembered by all. "Everything is very lovely, dear. The flower arrangements are exquisite."

"Oh, I'm so glad you like them." Lexy hiccupped loudly and I winced. "Excuse me." Lexy held her hand to her face. "It's such a pleasure to have you here. You don't know what a pleasure it is to have you here, Bady Lird." I bit my cheek but Michael laughed out loud and then Lexy started laughing. "I'm sorry, I guess I'm just a little star-struck. Please forgive me." Lexy hiccupped again and Mrs. Delgado moved forward, forcing Lexy to step aside. Lexy stood next to Michael, who rested one hand on her shoulder and the other on her waist to steady her.

"And this," Mrs. Delgado nodded her head toward me, "is David Thorpe, the young man who just made that major gift to the Wildflower Research Center."

Mrs. Johnson held my hand with both of hers as she greeted me. "Your letter and your generosity have touched my heart, David. I want you to know how grateful I am to you for endowing the new Karl A. Schumann Children's Botanic Playspace at the Center."

"You're very welcome. It's a real thrill to meet you, ma'am. I've always admired what you've accomplished for the state with your wildflower programs. You've made driving the highways each spring an outing in itself."

"Thank you, dear. That was just the beginning." She smiled broadly. "It was important to show the public the incredible diversity of beauty that's increasingly at risk." It was difficult for me to believe she was well into her eighties as she spoke with the directed passion of an articulate activist half her age. "That's why it is now so important that we are perceived as a research center of national prominence, and your gift certainly helps us in our mission to preserve native species, not just in Texas, but all over the country."

"I was happy to do it. I personally plan on learning a lot from the center, so it made sense for me to support it."

"That is so nice to hear. Please visit often, dear. Your passion and enthusiasm will always be welcome."

"Thank you, ma'am. I will remember this evening forever." I turned to Michael. "Well, we've been ignoring my old buddy over here long enough. "Mrs. Johnson, I'd like you to meet my friend Michael Laramie. He's the artist whose latest sculpture is being dedicated tomorrow on campus."

"How wonderful." Lady Bird shook hands with Michael. "How does it feel to achieve such success at such a young age?"

"Spectacular." Michael deepened his voice and held out his arms. "It makes me feel spectacular and magnificent and fabulous." We all laughed. "I'm sorry." He held his hand to his mouth. "I'm a little caught up in the evening. Like our friend Lexy here." He glanced at Lexy, who was standing next to him looking sheepish. We all looked at Lady Bird, expectantly.

"Well, it was very nice meeting you all. Enjoy this marvelous evening. You've all got so much to be proud of. And thank you again, David." She turned toward Mrs. Dunworthy and they, along with Mrs. Delgado, walked toward the head table.

When they were out of hearing range Michael looked over to me. "Why didn't you tell me you gave a bunch of money to that place?"

"Because I wanted it to be a surprise. Surprise." I smiled, picked up my half-filled plate from the table and began eating."

Lexy turned toward Michael and me. "Oh, my, God, was it as bad as I think?"

"Bady Lird?! Geez, Lex. That was a good one." I munched a basil garnish.

"Yeah, Lex. Even I almost coughed up a grape," Michael chimed in.

"I'll never hear the end of it from Delgado." She hiccupped. "I need a glass of water." She scanned the nearby tables.

"So you embarrassed her, so what? She heard the nice things Lady Bird . . . ."

"AKA, Bady Lird, the badest lird around," Michael blurted. Lexy and I ignored him.

"As I was saying." I cleared my throat. "She heard Mrs. Johnson compliment you on everything. That's all she really cares about." I wiped my forehead with the back of my hand.

"Oh God, David. I'm so embarrassed."

"Get over it." I smiled at her and rocked up and down on my heels and toes. "You always do."

"Oh God, I need to sit down." Lexy walked away with a slight limp.

I ate a few bites of a large poppy seed cracker and then set my plate on an empty table and looked toward the exit. "I'm going to go get some air. It's gotten sort of stuffy in here."

"Just a minute, I'll go with you." Michael wiped up the last bit of caviar from his plate with a piece of sourdough roll, stuffed it in his mouth, and then set his plate on the table near mine.

"No, no, that's okay. Why don't you go find Lexy—and please don't give her anymore shit. Try to make her feel better. I'll catch up with you guys in a while, okay?"

"Sure, but are you all right?"

"Definitely. I just feel like a little walk. I won't be long."

"Okay, sure." Michael walked in the direction that Lexy had gone and soon disappeared among groups of dancing people. I took my time walking through the room, looking into the individual faces of the well-heeled crowd and seeing a feigned ease etched into them all. I passed through the double mahogany doors and out into the hallway, and then took the stairs two at a time and left through the main entrance.

I removed my jacket even though it was cool out. As I walked west I noticed that the sky was almost completely dark, with blue deepening into black where the stars began to show. There was no breeze but the air smelled earthy and clean, like a cool front was beginning to come through from the northwest. I walked across an expanse of lawn to Red River Street and followed the sidewalks to East Campus Drive, before heading past the Performing Arts Center, above the fountain and toward the Fine Arts Library grounds. It took only five minutes to reach Michael's sculpture, which was mounted on a caramel colored marble base lodged into the earth. It stood between two mature live oak trees in the glow of distant lights, too faint to even cast a shadow.

I walked closer to the large bends of copper, which reached over eight feet tall and looked sort of like a twisted, three-dimensional bass clef. A series of various sized openings was bored into the thickest part of the piece. I walked around the sculpture, looking at it from all sides. I liked it much better than when I had seen it in Michael's studio. It seemed as if it had been somehow freed in the large expanse of college campus green—lawn, trees and shrubbery.

I felt as if Copper One had an attractive force, serving as a nucleus around which I was orbiting, held at a fixed distance but unable to break away. I looked at it from all angles as I continued the even pace of my circling. After several minutes I finally noticed an engraved copper rectangle set into the marble. I bent to look at it, but it was on the dark side of the sculpture and I couldn't even make out Michael's name. As I stood I noticed an intermittent breeze, rustling the mountain laurel leaves. The wind picked up and it smelled like fall and made my neck prickle. I stood back from the sculpture even before I heard its first low, wavering tones. And then others joined in and faded in varying combinations. I crouched down, smiling and felt a little sad.

"You recognize the sounds?"

I turned, startled, and saw Michael standing ten yards away from me nearer to the distant streetlight.

"God, you scared me." I stood up and walked toward him. "I wasn't even planning on coming here tonight, but . . . ."

"It's okay." Michael whispered below the voice of the sculpture. "Do you recognize the sounds?"

I listened intently, as we walked closer to the sculpture, and then a pleasant tingling flashed through my spine and I could barely speak. "Yes, I do."

"Like the doves we saw on that marsh."

Steadying myself, I lowered my voice to a whisper. "It really does sound like them." I turned and looked into Michael's eyes. "Everything, the whole effect, is beautiful."

"Man, David, I'm so glad you're into it. Your opinion means more to me than anyone's. I actually think it's my best work yet. And can you imagine, fifty thousand dollars? Last week it was trapped in my studio, and now, just listen."

"Yeah, it's pretty incredible." I kept my voice low. "Go ahead and tell me, what'd you name it? It's too dark to read the plaque. I admit, I already tried."

Michael bent down and grabbed a lighter from his pocket. He flicked it and cupped his hand around the flame. I leaned over his shoulder and saw the inscription: First Flight / Michael Laramie / September 22, 1990.

I stood up and ran my hand along the rising form of the smooth, dull copper. I turned and saw Michael standing a few paces back, watching me and smiling.

"Man, you are so handsome."

"Come here" was all I could say.

Michael walked over to me, and as we embraced he rubbed his hand up and down on the back of my sheared head, and whispered into my ear, "Ooooh, I love the feel of this."

12

Mrs. **Moody walked outside in her robe** and slippers
and bent over to pick up the newspaper that lay bulging in its
plastic bag on her front lawn.

"Good morning, Helen."

She turned quickly. "Oh David, you startled me. Good
morning. Well, it's already past noon, actually. I'm off to a
slow start today." She held the paper in front of her with both
hands. "What are you doing here on a Sunday?"

"I brought you the tulip bulbs I promised. I was in San
Antonio last week digging up Aunt Ivy's beds." I lifted a large
cardboard box out of the back of the Jeep. "I've been storing
them in sawdust at my house."

"Did you save some for yourself?"

"I kept enough. I can always get more next year."

"So you've decided not to sell your aunt's house?"

"I never really considered selling it. Right now, a neighbor's keeping an eye on things and watering the yards until I get an irrigation system installed." A car drove past the house, its window down with loud music playing.

"Let's walk around back. I don't like standing out here in my robe where just anyone can see me."

I followed Mrs. Moody around the side of the house, through the back gate, and onto the patio.

"Is it okay to plant the bulbs this early?" She looked at me, tilting her head.

"Probably, though it would be better to wait until it gets cooler."

"I think fall is just around the corner. Did you feel that front come through last night?"

"Yeah, it felt good, but I'm afraid it was just a tease." I began walking toward her garage. "I'll set these in here for now. I'll prepare the beds next week, but we can plant them whenever we want."

"That sounds like a good plan." Mrs. Moody shuffled toward her patio.

I returned from the garage and sat at the wrought-iron patio table next to Mrs. Moody. She had stripped the plastic off the newspaper and was looking at the front page.

"Oh David, I almost forgot to ask you. How was the big gala last night?"

"I wish you could have been there. It was a lot of fun. I even got to meet Lady Bird Johnson."

"Really? How exciting! Oh David, that's just marvelous. How is she doing these days?"

"She seems to be getting along very well. We talked briefly about her plans for the National Wildflower Research Center. Have you heard much about it? Its new big home is opening southwest of the city next spring."

"I read about it in the paper a while back. I'm anxious to take a tour."

"Me, too. We'll have to go together sometime."

"That's a good idea." Mrs. Moody folded the paper in half and turned it over. "So what have you been doing with your Sunday so far?"

"This morning I went to a dedication ceremony on campus for a piece of sculpture by my friend Michael. You remember him, he came with me to your birthday party?"

"Of course I remember. You two were the hit of the party. All my friends were asking about you. I think they were envious that I had such handsome young men as friends." Mrs. Moody laughed. "Especially Elaine. She was so disappointed that you wouldn't take on her gardening."

"It's not that I didn't like her."

"She understood. She didn't take it personally." Mrs. Moody reached over and pinched a spent rose blossom from a hybrid tea rose that grew next to the table. "So, what are you going to do with your afternoon?"

"Maybe do a little yard work around the house, maybe go shopping. And then later this afternoon I'm going to drive to New Braunfels. I'm thinking about going to a few antique shops."

"Oh how nice. I haven't been down to New Braunfels since Dr. Moody died." Her voice diminished and sounded wistful.

I stood and pushed my chair up against the patio table. "Well, Helen, I think I'm going to take off. I'll see you Tuesday morning."

"Now, you know it makes no difference to me when you come by." She stood up. "Just don't let a week go by without letting me know when I'll see you. I got worried about you last time when you didn't call."

"I know. I'm sorry about that. I promise to call if I can't make my regular schedule."

"Good, that makes me feel better. Well, you have a good time in New Braunfels." She patted me on the back as I started to walk to the gate.

"Thanks. I'll try."

* * *

"So, what type of gun are you looking for, son?" The man behind the counter spread his hands across the glass topped display case, resting his potbelly over its edge. His black hair was slicked back with an oily hair dressing.

"I'm not really sure." My eyes jumped around, focusing first on the row of rifles propped upright behind the counter before scanning the handguns that lay on green felt beneath the glass.

"Well, what do you want to use it for? Hunting? Personal protection?"

"I guess a little bit of both." I lightly drummed my fingers along the wooden edge of the handgun case and looked back and forth. "See, I recently inherited a farm up near Taylor," I lied, "and you must know about their rattlesnake problem up there."

"Of course. Those rattlers love them rocks 'round there." He stepped back from the counter, interlocked his fingers and stretched his thick arms. "So, you thinking, maybe a handgun? Or maybe a rifle? You could go either way, though you'd have better aim with a rifle."

"I'd like something that I could keep in my pickup, something that would fit in the glove compartment, or say, in this backpack." I pointed with my thumb to the strap on my shoulder.

"I guess you'll have to go the handgun route then. At least for snakes, you won't need much firepower. Save you a lot of money, to boot. I've got a good selection of .22's over here." He walked a few paces behind the counter toward the front of the store and placed his finger on the glass case, pointing to a dozen pistols arranged in four rows on similar green padding.

"I don't think a .22 will do. It wouldn't be impressive enough?"

"To snakes?" He looked up at me, his eyebrows raised.

I laughed. "I guess it wouldn't matter to them, huh? No, I was thinking more of my friends."

"Well then, maybe a .357 or a .45 might be more to your liking. I got just about anything you could want." He again walked behind the corner, but toward the back of the store, to another section of the display case.

"Which is the more powerful of the two?"

"Well, the .45 has a larger caliber, but they'll both do the job."

"Okay, show me what you've got in .45's?"

He spread out a brown velvet pad over the counter before unlocking and sliding open the back of the case. He lifted out a small pistol and placed it on the on the pad. "This is my Colt Compact. It's a good mid-range gun, made by Colt of course. I usually recommend this to new gun owners because it's a great value at $495, yet still a good weapon."

I picked up the gun, held it in my right hand and then passed it back and forth between my hands. "Show me your most expensive model?"

"That would be this Para Ordinance right here." He pointed to the longest barreled gun in the case. "It's my most expensive .45 right now. Sells for $869. But to be honest with you, I don't really like this gun. Look at it? It just don't look right, and you seem to be a man who appreciates the way things look. Here . . . ." He returned the smaller pistol to the case, pulled out a larger one, and set in on the velvet pad. "Now this, this one I think you'll really like. It's a limited edition, nickel plated Colt Combat Commander. Check out the detail on the handle."

I picked it up, noticing how much heavier it was than the first one, and looked at the nouveau Western pattern engraved in the polished metal handle. "Pretty cool. How much?"

"You're not going to believe it, but it's my last one and it's priced at only $846. And to top it off, I read in *Shooting Times* that its the last edition that'll be engraved like this. It'll be a collector's item someday, that's for sure. You can give it to your grandson."

"I was thinking more of giving it to my father."

The shopkeeper looked up at me. A bell jingled as the front door to the store opened. A woman of about twenty-five wearing a yellow, sleeveless jumper walked up to the counter near the cash register at the front of the store. She pushed her sunglasses up past her tanned forehead and rested them on top of her dark blonde hair. She glanced toward the shopkeeper and me, then bent over and perused the cases.

"Go ahead, take a closer look at it. See how it feels in your hand. I'm going to see what she wants." He motioned his head to the woman at the front of the store.

I ran my finger across its shiny barrel, leaving an uneven smear. I again picked up the gun, gripped it in my hand and leaned its barrel backward so that it rested on my forehead pointing toward the ceiling. I smiled, scratching at an itch on my head with the sight on the barrel tip, wondering what Michael would think if he could see me.

The cold metal of the gun warmed in my grip, and the longer I held it, the more natural it felt clasped in my hand. I turned away from the salesman and the woman and held the gun up in front of me at arms length with both hands, spreading my legs, aiming at a target on a back wall. Without realizing what I was doing, I squeezed the trigger and heard a low click. Though the salesman and the woman didn't even notice, the sound reverberated in my mind as if a shot had been fired. I set the gun back on the counter and stared at it, seeing a tiny, distorted image of myself reflected in the rounded cylinder. I stood, gazing into the image, hands by my sides, listening to the woman and the salesman.

"Howdy, Miss. How you doing today?"

"I'm doing fine, thanks. And you?"

"Couldn't be better. What can I do you for?"

"I want to buy a gun, for myself, but I've never had one before, so I don't really know what I'm doing."

"I wouldn't imagine you're a hunter?" He laughed.

"No, not really." She sounded nervous. "I'm looking for something small." She whispered loudly. "For protection."

"There's nothing wrong with that, ma'am. It's a mighty frightful world out there. See that boy down there? He's here for the same reason."

I turned and saw him point at me and hand her a flyer.

"Owning a gun's a big decision. "Here's a list of certified shooting instructors in Travis County. You'll need to take lessons in gun safety and proper usage—not to mention learning how to aim." He smirked.

"Of course, I'll make an appointment right away." She folded the paper twice and slipped it into her handbag. She removed her sunglasses and set them on the counter and sighed. "I hate to admit it, but I just don't feel safe anymore."

"There's no shame in that. So what size do you think you want?"

The woman's shoulders untensed and she smiled, leaning into the counter. "I want something small, something that I could keep in a purse if I needed to, but a small purse, a clutch, something like this." The woman set a greeting card size black leather purse with a matching shoulder strap on the counter. "I'm so sick of the violence out there, you know? My friend Jo Ann was attacked last week jogging in Zilker Park. I thought this was supposed to be a safe city?"

"There's danger everywhere, ma'am. It's a frightening fact of life. We just got to prepare for it, that's all." He spoke like he'd been saying the same lines all his life. "Now, as for a gun for you, the only ones that would fit in that bag would be these little .22s and .38s over here." He stepped to the left and pointed down. "See that .38 Special right there, that was the gun of choice for Police Woman's Angie Dickenson."

"Angie who?"

"Never mind."

"You know, I've already made up my mind. I'll take that one." The woman frenetically rubbed her hands together and nodded her head, smiling.

"Nice choice." He lifted out a tiny chrome-plated pistol whose handle was inlaid with abalone shell. "You do have a license, don't you?"

"Oh yes of course, here." She hurriedly pulled out a piece of paper from her purse and pushed it toward the salesman. She picked up the gun, which looked more like a Christmas tree ornament. "Look, it matches my ring." The woman held out her right hand and pointed to a large opal. She looked over to me. "Hey there, don't you think this gun looks good with this purse?" She gave me a flirtatious smile and lay the gun against the black leather handbag.

"It's truly amazing how good it looks." I tried to look sincere. "You should buy two. Maybe sleep with one under your pillow?"

"Now there's an idea. I never thought about that." She looked up at the shopkeeper. "How much are they?" I looked away, incredulous.

"Three-eighty-eight each."

"I think I'll just take the one today."

As she filled out paperwork, he also sold her a leather case for the .38 and a box of fifty bullets. He wiped off the fingerprints from her gun with a clean rag. "Good thing you decided to buy now. You never know when that waiting-period law will pass. You can start getting your peace of mind back as soon as you walk out the door. Now don't forget to make an appointment with one of those instructors right away." He slipped the gun into the leather case and zipped it closed. "Now those classes, that's what should be required."

Before the bell on the door rang upon the woman's exit, the man was again back over at my end of the counter. "Sorry that took so long. When you first walked in, you didn't strike me as the impatient type, but of course no one likes to wait."

"That's okay. I thought you were pretty quick, actually."

"Business has picked up so much lately that I'm thinking about making George full time. He only works for me a few afternoons a week and every other weekend."

"I didn't mind waiting, really. I've decided on this one." I slid the Combat Commander toward him along the felt pad.

"You can't go wrong with Colt." He licked his fingertip and pulled out a triplicate form. "I'll need to see your license for the gun and your driver's license. Go ahead and fill this out." He handed me a pen and began wiping down the Colt.

"Would you like some ammunition?"

"Huh?" I looked up, dazed.

"Some bullets, boy. For the gun."

"Sorry, yeah, of course."

"How many would you like? We got boxes of twenty, fifty, a hundred . . . ."

"Twenty's good."

I looked down at the form that I'd half filled. "How much of this information is required by law?"

"Not much yet. But it looks like the Legislature will be changing that come next session. I couldn't care less about it though. I've always wanted basic information on my customers anyway, so I can let them know when certain merchandise arrives. You know, sort of for personal marketing. Hell, I don't care who I sell a gun to. Business is business." He noticed me pulling out $100 bills from my wallet. "Especially cash business." We met each other's stare and he smiled.

As he walked to the register he continued talking, raising his voice in the distance. "I agree with registering information on my customers. If it can help solve crimes, I'm all for it. What I don't like is that damn seven-day waiting period they're talking about. It'll never pass, though. When a man wants a gun, he usually wants it right away. You know what I mean? We're not bred for delayed gratification." He laughed. "Maybe they should only require that for women. Ha. Would prevent a lot of dead husbands, I'd imagine."

"Yeah, I'd imagine."

* * *

I sat in my Jeep in the parking lot of the 7-11 on Seguin Street, looking at the cover photo on the New Braunfels street map I had just purchased inside, along with a bottle of Coke and a bag of peanuts. In the photo a young couple stood smiling, leaning over the railing of the white gazebo on the downtown plaza. Branches of flowering redbud trees cascaded into the shot, framing it on both sides. I unfolded the map and spread it out on the passenger seat, wondering if my father would be home and how he would react at seeing me. Would he be happy, I wondered, or angry? Would he even know who I was?

I ripped open the small plastic bag of peanuts and unscrewed the top of my Coke bottle. I looked at the street index and located Pecan Street, E-J, 14. I poured some of the peanuts into my mouth before locating the street on the map with my finger. Pecan ran into Walnut Avenue, which led to Seguin Street. I wasn't surprised to find out that I wasn't very far away. I finished the peanuts, lodged the Coke bottle between my legs, and started the ignition. I suddenly felt tired, and anxious about just showing up without calling first. I looked at my pack in the back seat and I reached to turn on the radio.

I followed the route, slowing my speed after I turned onto E. Pecan Street. The first house number I saw was 427, and then 431. I knew I was going the right way but directed my attention to the opposite side of the street. When I drove through an intersection to enter the six hundred block I glanced up the street and anticipated which house it would be. I saw the small, wood frame bungalow before I noticed the black 612 tacked above the front door. I drove past it, my heart pounding with the accelerated bass beat of a song on the radio, and I felt weak, hardly able to push in the clutch to shift gears. The image of the house was imprinted in my mind, its pale yellow paint peeling on the front porch, surrounding a wooden bench swing that hung from the ceiling of the front porch. A light blue Ford Fairlane was parked in the driveway alongside two pyracantha bushes, whose berries had already begun to turn orange.

I turned around at the next intersection and drove past the house again. I continued back onto Seguin Street, my heart slowing, trying to get used to the idea of actually seeing him. I drove downtown to the plaza, took the circle around to San Antonio Street and headed to Landa Park. I drove through the park, looking at the huge old oak trees along the Comal River. Light green fronds of Spanish moss hung from the branches and moved in the slight wind. I knew I'd go back. I had become too curious to forget about everything and drive back to Austin, a peanut wrapper and a half-empty Coke bottle all to show for my trip.

I drank from the bottle and left the park, tracing my route back to my father's house. I parked the car, slung my pack over my shoulder, and walked on the chipped and cracked sidewalk leading to the porch. I knocked on the wooden screen door, which rattled against its frame, its dangling hook jumping with every knock.

"Just a minute already, I'm coming for Christ's sake." His voice seemed different. It was still deep but not as threatening.

The door opened away from me and I saw him through the ripped screen, which had been patched with black thread sown through the delicate wires. It surprised me to see the small, gray-haired man standing on the other side. He wore a white t-shirt with a frayed collar tucked into belted blue jeans that hung loosely from his hips.

"What can I do for you?"

"Are you D. J. Thorson?"

"Yes, who wants to know?"

"D. J. Thorpe, *Junior.*" I stood, leaning against the door frame, clutching my hand around it's wooden surface to ground my nerve.

"David?" He squinted.

"Hey, Dad. It's been awhile, huh?" My heart was again pounding, harder than before.

He stared at me as if he were examining an important document, looking for its watermark. "Oh my God, David. It really is you, isn't it?" He fumbled at opening the screen door by its handle before pushing it open with his boot-clad foot.

"Yep, it's really me." I remained on the other side, not wanting to move.

"Come in, please." He held open the door wider, noticing my apprehension. "I thought you'd never want to see me again."

I walked across the threshold, somehow expecting to find filth and disorder. "I thought the same about you." I looked around the living room and was surprised at how clean and neat it was. Matching blue pin-striped pillows lay on the sofa and contemporary prints of local landscapes hung framed on the walls. He walked up to me and rested his hands on my shoulders. "My God, David, I can't believe you're really here, son. He moved his arms behind my back, pulled me into him, and hugged me. I felt limp, surprised at how natural it felt to have him embrace me. After several silent moments he pushed me back, holding me by my shoulders at arms length. "Man, look at you, look at what a strapping young buck you turned out to be."

"You sound surprised." I wriggled out of his grip and walked around the room.

"There's just so much I want to say that I don't know where to start. I'm so shocked to see you." He stood near the door, watching me as I paced with my pack still slung over my shoulder. "But I am glad you tracked me down."

"Don't ask me why I did it or what I expected to find, but I felt like I needed to see you. It's just that I thought you were still in prison . . . but then when I found out you'd been out for two years without trying to get in touch with me," I took in a deep breath, "I didn't know what to do." I looked away from him and walked over to the couch. "I don't know, I just had to see you. I just had to see you." I sat on the couch and leaned my pack against the coffee table before scrunching up my body and burying my face in folded arms.

"Oh God, David, please don't. I am so sorry for everything. More than I can ever say. Look, everything's going to be different now. It's going to be okay."

"Don't say that!" My face remained hidden.

"Okay, look. You've found me, and I don't want to disappoint you again. Things have changed." He sat beside me on the couch and placed his hand on my back. I recoiled at his touch and he removed his hand.

"Maybe you hate me, maybe worse. I don't know how you must feel. Everything was so long ago, which doesn't make it any less real, I know. But when you didn't respond to my first letter, and then when the others were returned unopened from your Aunt Ivy's house, I thought you didn't want anything to do with me ever again."

I'd always wondered if there had been other letters, but I didn't want the confirmation to make any difference. I remained as before on the couch, wanting to listen to him, but not wanting to see him speak.

He stood up and walked across the room as he talked, jangling the change in his pocket. "After a year without hearing from you I started to accept that I had lost you forever. I never blamed you for not writing me. I knew I wasn't a good father to you, so I was convinced that you were better off with your Aunt Ivy."

He walked back to the edge of the sofa, stepping off of a rug and straightening it with his foot. "Can I get you anything to drink? A soda? Some water? A beer?" He clutched at his shirt pocket as if he expected to find a pack of cigarettes there.

I shook my head, "No."

"I know we've both got a lot of things to say, but I need to tell you a couple of things up front." He sat on the couch.

"What things?" I sat up straight and looked at him, wandering what could be worse than I already knew.

"Well, for starters, I got married again after I got out of prison, and then, well . . . ."

We both looked up at the sound of a doorknob turning. A woman who appeared to be in her mid thirties walked in the room holding a baby. She looked toward my father. "Oh, I'm sorry D.J., I didn't know you were expecting company."

My father stood up. "Marilyn, this is my son, David. He just got here." He walked over to her. "And David, this is my wife, Marilyn—and our daughter, Laura."

Marilyn smiled slightly in my direction, looking a little confused. "It's nice to meet you David. Your father's told me a lot about you."

I smiled at her and nodded politely, thinking, what could he possibly know about me to tell? But I was unable even to say hello.

The baby looked at me on the couch and then reached her arms out toward her father, squeezing her fingers in tiny clenches. He took Laura from Marilyn, kissed her on the cheek, and carried her over to the couch where I was sitting. She began to cry.

"Laura Jane, this is your brother, David." He sat her on his lap and turned her toward me. "See, it's okay. He's a good guy, yes he is." The baby stopped crying for a moment and then started again, turning her head away from me and burying her face in my father's shirt.

"I'm sorry, David. We've been at a birthday party for one of her cousins. I think she's over tired and needs her diapers changed." Marilyn spoke to me in a soft voice as if I dropped by every Sunday afternoon. She walked over to my father and took Laura from him. "I'm going to go change her and put her down. I'm pretty worn out myself. I don't mean to be rude, but I think I'll take a nap, too, give you two some time alone. Nice meeting you, David."

She walked out of the room and my father again joined me on the couch.

"It looks like you've got your chance to start over." I leaned back into the couch, somehow feeling more comfortable after seeing my dad with his daughter.

"I've been very lucky. Marilyn has been good to me."

"And you, to her?"

"Yes, I have. I hope that's not too hard for you to believe."

"How'd you meet her?"

"I shared a cell with her brother in Huntsville. He always showed me the letters and photos she sent him. After he was paroled—let's see, it was about three years before I got out—she began writing me." He leaned forward, as if to stretch out his back. "She eventually started visiting me and later, after I was able to leave the halfway house in Taylor, we got married and moved here." He looked down. "Laura was born less than a year later."

"Instant assimilation, new family and all. I guess you have been pretty lucky."

"I'm lucky to have them, David. Marilyn's a great mother. She knows everything about my past, including you and your mom and all my problems, and even the truth about my crime, and she still loves me."

"I guess I should be happy for you." I glanced at a framed watercolor print of the Comal River running through Landa Park hanging on the wall above my father. "What do you mean, 'the truth about my crime'?"

"I just mean she knows everything about me—the good, the bad and the ugly. Only there wasn't much good in my past, I'll admit." He shifted his weight on the couch and rested his head against his arm. "We can talk more about all these things later. How have you been?"

I looked down at my backpack sitting upright near me on the floor, watching as it slid along the scuffed wooden leg of the coffee table, just about ready to fall.

"Hey D.J, what's the good word?" The man behind the bar wore a plain white t-shirt with the sleeves cuffed, revealing tanned, muscled arms. My dad had suggested we walk to this neighborhood beer joint to talk further.

"Don't know one." My father looked over to me. "Jake, I'd like you to meet my son, David." The bartender reached his arm across the wooden bar top and shook my hand.

"Glad to know you. What can I get for you?" Jake planted his hands on the bar, his arms set in a wide stance, eyebrows raised.

"A Bud, bottle would be great."

"A bottle of Bud for the young man it is." He looked at my dad. "I didn't know you had a son, D.J.?" He reached into the beer box beneath the bar and retrieved a Miller Lite, opened it and set it in front of my dad, and did the same with a Budweiser for me.

"David's all grown up and living in Austin now. He decided to drive down to surprise me this afternoon." Dad took a sip from his beer and looked toward me.

"Well, that's a nice surprise. Let me know if I can get you anything else. I'll get out of your way to let you two gents visit." Jake walked away to the far side of the bar and then leaned over a newspaper spread out over the wide wooden bar.

I swiveled back and forth on my stool, looking around the large room, which was dimly lit by several neon beer signs. The floor was worn hardwood, swept but never cleaned. Booths upholstered in dark red vinyl were attached to three sides of the room, and there were a few round tables closer to the bar. There was no one else in the place.

"What's the deal with the new name, D.J.? I've been meaning to ask." I picked up the bottle and poured almost half the beer down my throat with the first drink.

"Even though my trial was over fifteen years ago, I didn't want to take the chance of people making the connection, especially in a town that gets the San Antonio papers. Anyway, I decided to go by my initials, and I took Marilyn's last name when we got married. She's not from here either, so no one's ever questioned it." Dad spread his fingers flat on the bar and began pressing them one at a time against the wood surface. "Anyway, I decided to look for work at a place where I thought they wouldn't be too curious about my past."

"So what *do* you do?" I watched his fingers continue the pressing pattern: thumb, index, middle, ring, pinky.

"I work at an old hardware store near downtown. The widow of the original owner hired me. I'm basically a sales clerk, but I unload the delivery trucks and do some stocking. I work part time and have the weekends off." He quickened the pace of his finger movements. "I pick up Laura from day care at noon and stay with her at home during the afternoons. Marilyn's the real breadwinner. She's got a good job at the post office, insurance and everything."

My dad lifted up his almost empty bottle and tilted it toward Jake, trying to get his attention. Jake noticed and set up another round. Dad then stood, picked up the two bottles and motioned for me to follow. I picked up my pack from beside my stool and followed him to the farthest booth, whose tabletop was hidden from Jake's view. We sat across from each other and sipped from our beers for a minute, avoiding eye contact. It seemed as if he would have been content to sit with me all afternoon, drinking beer and saying nothing.

When he started rotating his bottle, scraping its bottom on the worn wooden table, I reached over to stop the noise.

"Look, I guess I'm real happy for you and all, the way everything seems to be working out with your life. I know it must've been rough being locked up all those years." I drank from my beer. "But I don't like the fact that it's been so easy for you to forget that you have a son." I lifted my pack up onto the table to my right.

"I never forgot about you, David. I've already explained about the letters . . . ."

"Yeah, I know. But how could you just give up, especially after you got out of jail? I still don't understand why you didn't try to find me."

"You're right. I guess I was trying too hard to build a new life and forget about my past and . . . ."

"And since I was part of that past, you could just forget about me, like that." I snapped my fingers. "I wish it was that easy for me to forget about you."

"David, we have a chance to start over now. Why can't we just put the past behind us?"

"You know, I did try to forget as well, but somehow it hasn't come as easy for me as it has for you." I pulled my pack closer to me.

"What do you keep in that thing?" He motioned to the pack with the bottom of his beer bottle as he took a drink.

"Stuff." I looked disinterested and started remembering what it was like living with my parents as a kid, all the anger, the yelling, the fighting.

"You sound like a kid: 'Stuff.'" He smiled. "What kind of stuff?"

"Books, a water bottle, paper, pens, a gun. Stuff like that."

"A gun? You're kidding?"

"Yeah, I'm kidding." I drank from my beer bottle, watching him scoot back in his seat and look around the vacant room.

"You know, Dad. I was really scared of you after Mom died. I hated that you had been so mean to her." It was hard for me to speak.

"I wasn't mean to your Mom, David." He glanced at my hand clutching the bottle in front of me.

"Come on, Dad. I heard all the yelling and cursing, and all the things you'd blame her for and accuse her of."

"All married couples argue, David. I know I had quite a bad temper . . . ."

"You know you used to really scare me. You scared us all the time with your threats and your cursing. Do you remember what it feels like to be scared, Dad?" I reached over and unzipped my pack.

"Of course I do. For chrissakes I spent fifteen years of my life in prison. It doesn't get much scarier than that."

I pulled the pistol out of my backpack and slid it across the table, then placed my hands over it in front of me.

"So, you do have a gun. "Jake!" My father called out to the bartender, who I had just seen go into the men's room. There was no response.

"No need to be afraid, Dad. I'm not going to do anything stupid. I don't want to take after you and end up in prison."

He raised his eyebrows, took a deep breath, and drank from his beer, all the while looking like he was ready to bolt. But instead he took a deep breath and continued speaking, more quietly. "I'm just surprised; you didn't seem to like guns much as a kid."

"I don't like them, but I'm glad you taught me how to use them. I just bought this one today." I uncovered my hands. "It's a .45, a Colt."

"I see that."

"A Colt Combat Commander. Isn't it nice?"

"It looks very nice. Why do you have it here, now?" His voice became more uneven.

"Maybe I thought I needed to protect myself. Or, maybe I wanted to scare you."

"Well, you've scared me. Now, would you mind putting it away?"

"Why'd you do it, Dad? Why'd you treat Mom so bad? You know, I used to want to kill you when you'd lay in to her." He winced and looked away. "Yeah, she never had a bruise, but you beat her down Dad, you made her sick." I picked up the gun.

"David. Come on, put that down. Your Mom got leukemia. No one knows why."

"We just wanted you to love us."

"I did love you both, and I still love you. I just had so many problems back then. I won't deny how I acted, and I'm so sorry for it now." He shifted his weight back and forth in his seat, looking toward the bathroom for Jake. "David, I understand how you feel, and I want to prove . . . ."

"Are you scared now?" I slid the safety off the gun and cocked it.

"I already told you, I'm scared. I don't know why you're doing this." His forehead and face had begun to sweat.

I pointed the gun at him and pulled the trigger to the click of an empty chamber.

"Shit, David, are you crazy?" He breathed hard, and I noticed a breeze through an open window carrying the scent of cedar trees from the north.

"I think we're all a little crazy, but I'm not crazy enough to kill you." I put the gun back into my pack.

"Christ, David. You scared the holy shit out of me."

"Good." I shed any remaining bravado, started to shake, and lowered my voice. "I want you to mean the things you just said, Dad. I want to believe them." I looked away from him for a moment and then stared into his face, my eyes starting to well. "I do believe that you loved Mom and me, Dad. And I've seen enough of your life, especially with Laura, to believe that you have changed."

"I have, and in spite what you just pulled, I did mean what I said. And I want you to be a part of Laura's life, and mine of course, if you'll want to." He breathed deep and wiped his forehead. "But if that's going to happen, you're going to need to know a lot more about me, and accept what you learn. I've pledged to be totally honest with Marilyn and Laura for the rest of my life, and I want to extend that promise to you."

"Sounds like a good policy for everyone, huh?" I saw Jake walk back to his station behind the bar.

"Some of the stuff may be pretty hard to hear, but that's just the way life is. You deal with shit, and then you move on. Because if you don't move on, you never move past the shit."

He glanced at my pack. I zipped it closed and dropped it under the table.

"Geez, I could use another beer. You?" He nodded to me, and I shook my head no, and then he raised his voice. "Hey Jake, another Lite over here."

"This honesty thing, you're going to tell me about killing that man, huh? I'm not sure I want to hear it all, but I am curious about a few things." Jake brought Dad's third beer and took away the empties. "After I moved in with Aunt Ivy, I read everything in the newspapers. Aunt Ivy hid the daily paper from me, but I bought my own copy every day after school at the HEB down the street. I even clipped out the articles, so that I could re-read them."

"So you only know what the journalists have told you."

"But why did it happen, Dad? Was it really an accident?"

He drank from his beer and looked into my eyes, as if he didn't know how to begin. "It goes without saying that you and I don't know very much about each other. Your last memory of me was seeing me taken away by the police, and I hardly remember you as a twelve year old. I remember you as a little boy, but later it seemed like I slipped from your life, letting your mother raise you." He began picking at the label on his sweating beer bottle. "The last time you and I saw each other I was thirty-six years old. I had a well-paying job, but there was always so much pressure at the firm. You probably only remember that I was hardly ever home. I always thought it would get better, but it never did. I worked every evening and almost all weekends.

"And then, after your mom died, I didn't know how I was going to take care of you without her. Things eased up at the firm, only temporarily because my boss was sympathetic about Vivian, but then it was the same old thing. You were old enough so that you didn't need a babysitter, and I felt really bad about being gone. I just became angrier and angrier at everyone and everything, blaming God for all that seemed wrong in my life. I knew I had treated your mother badly, and that made me feel worse. I didn't know how I was going to be a father to you after she died."

"So then you found someone to kill just so you wouldn't have to?"

"No David, it wasn't like that. Bob Grimes was a new guy in our department. He was bright but still wet behind the ears, like a kid, you know? Our managing partner saw him as the future of the firm. I wasn't even friends with the guy, but I was friendly. He was always coming in my office to ask me questions, and then would end up going off on a tangent and taking up my time, which irritated the hell out of me because the guy just couldn't take a hint." He drank from his beer. "One afternoon at the office, he had been talking about growing up in a small town and how he missed being out in the country. I figured, okay, maybe I do have something in common with this bumpkin. He said he liked to hunt and owned several guns, so I invited him to go dove hunting with me one weekend." Dad drank from his beer. "It's hard to talk about this, let alone be telling you."

"I can imagine, but you've already started." I saw Jake coming toward our booth with two bottles of beer.

"These are on the house, guys. It makes me feel good seeing a father and son together; reminds me of my own little boy. Unfortunately, he lives with his mom in Dallas."

"That's real nice of you Jake. Thanks." Dad tipped his bottle to him.

"Yeah, thanks," I added, not wanting the free beer.

"Enjoy." Jake walked back to the bar.

"Okay, so this was the weekend when Bob was killed right?" I prompted him.

Dad nodded.

"So, were the newspapers right about the way the accident happened?"

"It wasn't an accident."

"So, it was self defense then?"

"No, David, it wasn't."

I clutched my beer bottle tightly and dragged it across the table toward me as the hair prickled on the back of my neck. "What do you mean?"

"Bob Grimes didn't have a malicious bone in his body. He never knew that I was transferring the funds. And that prosecutor, he was way off base. Bob wasn't blackmailing me. He actually liked me, sometimes I think a little too much, but didn't have a clue about the embezzling. I never even spent the money. I just took it to see if I could get away with it. I made it look like a computer error and then paid back the firm every penny without anyone being the wiser." Dad leaned forward across the table, an edge of anger in his voice. "But then there we were, alone on our boss's ranch, which was miles from the nearest farmhouse." He drank from his beer bottle. "This is so hard to admit to my own son, but I had always had this strong compulsion."

"What sort of compulsion?"

He lowered his voice. "To see what it would look like, in real life, to see a man blown away with a shotgun at close range."

"Come on, Dad. Now *you're* scaring *me*. You do realize how sick that is?" I sat up straighter and pulled my feet toward me under the bench seat of the booth.

Of course, I know. I had tried to put it out of my mind, but it always crept back, stronger than before. But I'm not the same person I was fifteen years ago, and that's why it's so important for me to be telling you this. I can't hold anything back if we really want to start over. Remember the honesty we talked about earlier?"

"Sure, but we're talking about murder here. Do you know how hard it is hearing you confess to killing that guy?"

"I know, David." He leaned his head forward and shook it slowly from side to side. "It was terrible and sick, but it's the truth. The one thing I'd like you to keep in mind is that despite my lies, I was convicted of that crime and served fifteen years in Huntsville."

"But all that doesn't bring Bob Grimes back."

"I know, David. It was an insane thing to do, but a jury would have never believed an insanity plea either."

"All these years I wanted to believe that it was an accident, that you couldn't have been capable of intentionally killing him."

"I know, David. I've always felt worse about its effect on you than anything else. But only by knowing the truth can we really be free to start over."

"How could you do it? How did it happen?" I tugged at the collar of my shirt, thinking about the unloaded gun in my pack and my earlier stunt.

"I swear it was something I didn't plan. I was really looking forward to going hunting with someone. I knew you never liked going, which is why your gun thing just now scared the holy hell out of me. Plus, you know, it's different when you're going with your kid. Bob and I could take beer and talk about grown-up things." He resumed picking at his beer bottle label. "Well, anyway, we were on our way back to the truck after a morning without even seeing one dove. I was disappointed and frustrated and Bob was grumbling. I felt like I never wanted to leave that place. I never wanted to go back to work. I never wanted to go home again. I never wanted to have to be responsible for you again. I felt so trapped and so dead. And whenever I felt like that I would have those thoughts. And there I was having those thoughts for the first time with a gun. Bob had leaned his gun against the barbwire fence before beginning to crawl between the wires of the fence. And there he was, and there was his gun. I grabbed it, slid the safety off, and as he turned, I pulled the trigger." Dad closed his eyes tight. "God, David. You can't picture how horrible it was. There was never any of my imagined satisfaction in it, having acted on that compulsion. I immediately became sick by what I saw. And when I realized I had actually done it, that it wasn't only in my mind anymore, I panicked. I knew there was no way to hide what I'd done, and of course Bob had been killed instantly, so I wiped my prints off the gun with my shirt and lay it on the ground next to

Bob. I ran to the truck and drove to the nearest farmhouse and called for help.

"I was amazed at how sympathetic the sheriff was to me, saying how unfortunately common these incidents are in rural areas. I'm sure I was suspect from the beginning, but my story seemed credible. Only it really wasn't. But with no eyewitnesses and little reliable forensics testimony, the jury had to go on their gut feelings, and of course, they were right." Dad finished his beer. "And the rest, you already know."

"God, Dad. I can't believe you really killed him on purpose. Aunt Ivy was right."

"I can't believe it now either. But the fact was that I couldn't undo pulling that trigger. It took years afterwards in prison before I could train my mind not to constantly think about Bob or what I had done. And like I've said, I am remorseful, I served my time, but I can't let that one act determine my future anymore than it already has. So now that I've told you, like I've only done with Marilyn, I hope you can still accept me."

"You know, in some weird way it's easier for me to accept what you've just told me than for me to accept how you treated mom and me. You didn't just hurt her. I know you thought I never heard you, but I did; all those times late at night when you'd get really drunk and say things to Mom about me growing up to be a faggot." I looked at his eyes and saw them turn downward.

"God, I know, David. I'm so sorry for that. Not only because you heard it, but because I said it. Like I've said, I had so many problems back then. I was insensitive and ignorant about so many things and . . . ."

"But you were right."

He looked up at me suddenly.

"But I prefer the word 'queer.'" I smiled, trying not to cry. "It's true, Dad. I am gay."

He looked at me, surprised, and didn't say anything for a minute. Then he looked into my eyes. "Are you happy?"

"I've just recently begun to accept it, but yes, definitely, I'm very happy. I'm pretty excited about the way my life is finally turning out."

"David, who am I to judge anyone? I know it was tough for you growing up. Now I only regret that your mom's death and my actions made it worse. As long as you're happy . . . ."

"I've been dreading telling this to you all my life, even before I really knew there was anything to tell. I thought you would hate me even more than I thought you already did."

"I could never hate you. I know it's hard to believe, but I've always loved you.

13

I woke from a deep sleep to the sound of Abby's tail thumping against the rug next to my bed. She was sitting on her haunches and staring at me as I blinked open my eyes. I felt rested and content, my mind feeling clearer than it had for months. I reached over to pet Abby and looked at the clock on my night stand—ten o'clock. I stretched long and slow, not believing I had slept twelve hours. The room felt cooler than usual and I noticed the open window and smiled, realizing that a norther had blown through during the night, leaving its crisp autumn smell in my bedroom. I pulled up my light summer bedspread, which I had kicked off during the night and patted my hand on the bed for Abby to join me. She ignored my request, remaining sitting on her haunches wagging her tail. I knew she wanted me to let her out, but I felt so comfortably warm and tired, despite my long sleep. She began with noiseless mouth movements, as if she were saying, "Please, please get your lazy ass out of bed," and then started a crescendo of muffled but insistent barks.

I got up, wearing only a pair of white briefs, walked to the kitchen and let her out, pausing at the open door to enjoy the bright coolness of the morning. I returned to bed and yawned, closing my eyes. I felt a muscular tiredness throughout my body but also energized and somehow excited. When I opened my eyes I saw Lexy standing in the doorway. "Geez Lex, you startled me."

"I brought over some coffee—you sure look like you could use some. I also stopped by Sweetish Hill and picked up some scones."

"Thanks, Lex. How come you're not at work?"

"I left a message on Mrs. Delgado's voicemail over the weekend that was going to take today off." She laughed. "Today and every other day."

I sat up in bed. "You quit!?"

"Yeah. How could I follow Saturday night?"

"You *were* in top form, I have to agree." I pulled the cover over my chest.

"Yeah, well, that place has been stressing me out lately. I'm going to wait tables for a while and see what happens." Lexy took a sip from the navy blue travel mug she'd brought with her.

"That's a pretty bold move. I'm proud of you."

"Yeah, well I'm way behind on bold moves in my life. Anyway, I don't want to talk about my employment, or lack thereof, on such a beautiful morning. It's so nice out, I can't believe you of all people are still in bed."

"Isn't it great? I noticed the nip when I let Abby out earlier. I was just getting ready to jump in the shower. I've got to pick up Michael in about an hour. We're heading out to the farm."

"Oh, yeah. I forgot. Well, then hurry up so we can talk on the patio for a few minutes." She turned and started to walk toward the door. "I'm going outside to play with Abby."

Lexy was sitting at the patio table, sipping her coffee and watching Abby chase birds near the large fig tree in the far corner of the yard, when I walked outside. She set her mug down on the glass-topped table and looked up at me. "Talk to me."

175

"About what?" I sat in the chair next to her, wearing old jeans and a gray sweatshirt worn thin from a decade of washing.

"What do you mean 'about what?'?" What happened with your dad yesterday?"

"It was pretty bizarre, Lexy, but it went okay. I know it sounds weird, but I just needed to see him and know that he didn't hate me." I leaned back, balancing on the back legs of the chair.

""Why would you think he would hate you?"

"Oh, I don't know. There could be lots of reasons." I set my chair back on all four legs.

"Anyway, the important thing is that you're okay."

"Well, I wouldn't go that far, but it's a start. I've still got a lot to process."

"Are you planning to keep in touch with him?"

"Probably not a lot, but maybe more than I had thought because . . . guess what?"

"What? Come on, David. You know I don't like to guess. What?!"

"I've got a baby sister."

"You're kidding?"

'No, my dad got married again and has a daughter. Her name's Laura and she's about a year old."

"That's pretty exciting." Lexy paused to read my face. "It is, isn't it?"

"Of course it is, and I'd really like to be a part of her life somehow. My dad and his wife Marilyn want the same thing, so I guess I'll be seeing him more too."

"I'm glad you want to be close to her. She's pretty lucky to have such a strong, handsome, kind big brother."

"Oh, get out."

"And there's a certain look in your eyes that I haven't seen in years. You look, like, relaxed, like you're not just about to become a serial killer."

"Was I that bad?"

"That was supposed to be a compliment. You look, I don't know, happy."

I laughed. "You know, for the first time since I was about eight years old, I think I am. It feels odd." I smiled and drank from the coffee Lexy had poured for me.

"Face it, David, you've got a lot of things to be happy about. You just found your dad and learned you have a sister, the man you love is in love with you, you're rich as all get out, and most important of all, you have me as your best friend."

"Geez, Lex, you can be a real sweetheart when you want to be."

"My friend Beth says I need to start showing my softer side more often, but I've always thought that it was weak."

"Well you know what they say, Lex. The weak shall inherit the earth."

"That's 'meek,' David. The meek shall inherit the earth. It's from the Bible, you idiot."

I held my mug with both hands and drained the last bit of coffee. "I hate to be rude—because you know we're having this tender moment and everything." I smiled and Lexy rolled her eyes. "But, I've got to get going and pick up Michael."

"Can I hang out here a while?"

"Sure. Stay as long as you want, but I'm taking Abby with me."

"That's okay. I just love being in your backyard. I'm getting so tired of my apartment. I've been thinking about buying a house."

"Really?"

"But since I'm now officially unemployed, I don't think it's going to happen." Lexy poured more coffee. "Jack has been talking about us getting a place together, but I'm not sure." Lexy looked up at me, as if she wanted my opinion.

"Go for it, Lex. Remember what I was talking about the other day—everything involves risk. But it's the only way you can get a payoff. You know, I read this graffiti the other day and . . . ."

"God, David, I think you spend too much time in public restrooms."

"No thanks, I'm not going that route." Lexy looked at me, confused. "No, it was near the bulletin board in the Student

Union. It said: people tend to regret the things that they don't do more than the things they do do."

"Do do?"

"Think about it."

"I guess there's no harm in talking to him about living together."

I looked around the yard—the big oak tree in the center, the old pecan and fig trees to the right, and the younger crepe myrtles I had planted along the back fence. "What the hell, I'll give you my house if you want it. Then you and Jack can live here. I'm thinking about moving anyway."

"Really? Where?" Lexy sat up straighter.

"Oh, I don't know for sure. I've got all kind of possibilities swimming around in my head right now."

"You mean you'd really give me your house?"

"Sure, why not? Then I know I'll always be welcome here, and that it'll be in good hands."

"Wow, David, that's so generous. I can't believe you're serious." Lexy smiled, raised her eyes, and sipped her coffee. "There's just one other thing . . . ."

"Yes?"

"Will you still take care of the yards?" She smiled.

I wadded up the paper napkin that had been under my coffee mug and threw it at her. It bounced off her chin and landed in her lap, before falling off onto the patio and being swept off by a sudden breeze.

* * *

Michael stood next to the open grave and looked down at Aunt Ivy's coffin. He wore faded jeans ripped at both knees and a blue and green plaid flannel shirt. "The guy did a good job. Neat edges and it looks like six feet, doesn't it?"

"Oh, it is." I glanced at the soil piled to the right of the grave. "He must've just left; the dirt has hardly begun to dry." Sunset Memorial had coordinated the exhumation with an independent contractor. I'd mailed him a key to the farm, so he could prepare the grave. I had marked the plot with stakes, forming a long rectangle a few feet from Karl's gravesite.

"So we've just got to fill it in, right?" Michael walked around the perimeter, peering down at the white coffin, whose lacquer coat was marred and beginning to wear off. "I've been to my share of funerals, but I've never seen a coffin lying at the bottom of a grave before."

"Here." I handed him a shovel. "Start filling. I'm going to start digging up Karl's grave." I stood near the small cement cross and surveyed the dead and dying stalks of the wildflowers and the later flowering plants that filled Aunt Ivy's meadow each spring and summer. I remembered seeing the magical meadow at its peak for the first time that April when I was fourteen and Aunt Ivy showed it to me. Suddenly, I felt the same sudden feverish, prickly buzzing in my body that I had before. The barely perceptible tingle raced up and down my spine as the sense memory washed over me. I smiled in humble amazement, steadying myself for the sacred duty ahead of me.

"You've got the creepier job, that's for sure," Michael said, breaking me from my reverie.

I reeled in my distant gaze and looked down to where I was supposed to be on task. "But there was never anyone buried here. It's just like digging a hole to plant a tree. Besides I'm not even going to go that deep, only two or three feet."

"Isn't there some rule about six feet?"

"Yeah, but I think it's just a tradition, probably starting because of health code reasons in cities. But I'm not burying a body, just a few bones."

"This is true." Michael continued shoveling the dirt into the deep hole. "Hey, where's Abby?"

"She was snouting around the middle of the meadow a few minutes ago." I looked around and then pointed. "She's over there on the coastal Bermuda patch, probably heading toward the smells of the pond. She loves it out here."

"Yeah, looks like she's in dog heaven." Michael smiled. "It's a pretty big back yard."

Wielding our shovels in silence, Michael continued filling in Aunt Ivy's grave while I dug in front of Karl's marker. The breeze blew through the leaves of the hackberry trees that lined the barbwire fence separating the wildflower meadow from the hay field and the pond. The leaves sounded dry, as if they were tired from the overly long Texas summer and ready to fall.

After I'd dug a hole a little more than two feet deep, I noticed the soil seemed suddenly more fertile, and then I remembered the oak coffin Uncle Otto had built. I imagined that he and Uncle August hadn't dug a very deep grave and the coffin had probably decomposed decades before, adding to the richness of the soil. I figured I'd gone deep enough, but I scooped one last shovelful of soil and tossed it on top of the small mound near where Michael was standing.

"What's that?" Michael stuck his shovel into the soil and pointed to something shiny on top of the mound.

I dropped my shovel and knelt near the mound and grabbed a small chain whose links were clogged with damp soil. "Whoa, Michael! It's the bracelet I told you I saw in the picture of Karl I found at Aunt Ivy's house."

Michael took it from me and looked at it up close. "I remember. You thought you might've found it in the pond."

"Uncle August must have buried it in the empty coffin."

"What do you think that means?"

"Maybe Aunt Ivy asked him to bury it with Karl. I don't know." I shook my head, walked over to a large water bottle and washed the dirt from the bracelet. I dried it on the inside of my sweatshirt, polishing it on the worn fleece like fabric. The chain of heavy gold links measured about five inches long. Mud filled the tiny lettering of the inscription on the clasp. It read: To Baby Karl, Love, Aunt Clara and Uncle Otto. "Or maybe . . . oh, I don't know. It doesn't matter." I took off the navy blue baseball cap I'd been wearing, set it upside down on the ground, and placed the bracelet inside.

"What are you going to do with it?"

"I'm going to rebury it along with the bones. Don't you think that would be appropriate?"

"Sounds like an excellent idea."

"Looks like you're almost done." Aunt Ivy's grave was filled, level with the ground. "Go ahead and mound the rest of the dirt on top." I walked to the Jeep and carried out a small cardboard box on top of which lay the mesh bag containing Karl's remains.

"What's in the box?"

"Tulip bulbs from Aunt Ivy's garden. I'm planting some in Karl's grave."

"That's cool." Michael patted the oblong, rounded mound on top of Aunt Ivy's grave with his shovel blade. "What color are they?"

"Deep red. They were her favorite." I set the box down next to Karl's open grave and looked out across the meadow. In the far distance, I saw Abby running toward us, her pace slower than before. "You'll see them next spring. They'll be blazing in stark contrast to what you'll see out there." I pointed to the unsightly tangle of brown and green in the distance.

"I can't wait to see the meadow then, after hearing you talk so much about the wildflowers."

"It's pretty incredible. I'm thinking about building an apiary out here, probably on the edge of the meadow, over there." I pointed to a distant point near where the meadow joined the coastal Bermuda field.

"Since when do you want to keep birds?"

"Not an aviary, an apiary. I want to keep bees."

"Bees?"

"Yeah. They're great to have around, keeping everything pollinated and blooming."

Michael shrugged his shoulders and joined me as I knelt next to Karl's grave. I placed the bones as I imagined they would have lain naturally, as the last ones to decay into the earth. I positioned the skull piece first and then the two pelvic bone fragments closer to the foot of the grave. Michael picked up the bracelet from out of my cap and handed it to me, and I arranged it in a small circle between the bones. We stood and Abby ran up to us, panting. Michael filled her bowl from a water bottle and she lapped noisily, before walking around the mounds of damp earth, nose to the ground.

Michael sat a few feet away from me. "Come on, Abby. Come to Uncle Michael." He patted his hands on his thighs. I turned to him and smiled as I watched Abby walk over and lie next to him, emitting a satisfied grunt, as she settled her body into the damp earth.

I covered the bones and bracelet with enough soil to fill the grave more than half way. I opened the cardboard box, removed a smaller box filled with organic fertilizer for the tulip bulbs, and poured it into the rich, moist soil. I mixed it into the soil with my hands and formed a flat, oval surface on which to set out the bulbs. Michael and Abby sat nearby, watching me as if taking part in a communal ritual.

I picked out the two dozen tulip bulbs and pressed their bottoms into the fertile mixture. I shoveled the remainder of the soil over the bulbs, taking care not to knock them over until they were safely hidden. I patted the mound on top of Karl's grave as Michael had done with Aunt Ivy's.

Michael, Abby and I sat on the ground next to the sealed graves. The breeze was cool through the bright South Texas sunshine. Abby lowered her head, sighed and closed her eyes. Michael and I took her cue and closed our eyes and bowed our heads.

"Come on, faster." I ran ahead of Michael and Abby.

"Okay, okay," Michael panted. "Abby's been running all day, you know. We'll catch up with you, go on ahead."

I slowed my pace as we ran along the dirt road that curved through the woods, which separated the meadow from the creek valley. I was energized by the cool weather and the promise of fall and winter to come, a long winter to be indoors more often, to daydream and to plan.

When we reached the creek, we stopped, and Abby stood on a low rock and drank from the clear, flowing water.

"Is this why you were in such a hurry to get here, so that she could have another drink?"

"No, I want to show you up there." I pointed above the slope to the other side of the creek. "Come on." I looked at Abby standing on the rock, her nose pointing into the wind, wriggling, water dripping from her snout and being absorbed into the porous sandstone. "She's had enough."

Michael and I jumped from rock to rock to cross the creek while Abby walked through the shallow water.

"Oh hell, what's up there?" Michael sounded apprehensive. "Not another dreaded family secret, God forbid." He laughed.

"Nothing like that. Besides there aren't any more family secrets." Not bad ones anyway, I thought, looking forward to the exhilarating spell cast by wildflower fever each year. I imagined the following spring, running through the soft, surreal meadow so full with blue and white and yellow and pink and lavender, sharing it with Abby, and with Michael.

I looked up to see the blue sky drawn high with white wisps and smelled the loamy earth below. My entire body tingled again in anticipation of the power of the fever, as if it already had its grip on me. I tried to speak but I couldn't. I managed to walk a few paces toward a sloping live oak tree and leaned my body against it. My eyes closed as I slumped to the ground and I felt as if I'd gone somewhere else, carried along by the flowing water of the creek or soaring on a warm thermal with a flock of doves.

Michael walked up to me as I started to stand up and steady myself against the tree. "Are you okay?"

"I'm fine. I just got a little dizzy. Maybe I'm just too excited, or a little delirious or something." I resumed walking up the trail. "I was just daydreaming, and sort of got carried away." My head cleared further and I began to walk faster.

"Just watch your step. It looks tricky up ahead."

Michael followed as I climbed through a ravine lined with jagged rocks, which channeled rainwater from the above pastures into the creek. Near the top of the ravine, rocks gave way to a black soil and the beginning of a cattle trail. We ducked under low branches as we walked through the thicket that formed between the large, twisted live oak trees and the straight trunks of old cedar elms. The trail ended where another scattering of rocks lay, similar to the ones along the creek but high above the valley.

We stood on one of the flat rocks and looked down toward the creek, which was almost completely hidden from view by small trees and low-spreading shrubs.

"It's a much clearer view through there in the winter." I pointed toward the creek. "But I'm still going to clean out the goat-hangers and some of the other underbrush."

"There are oaks up here on top too, huh?" Michael pointed to a tree and walked around the area, away from the side that looked over the valley.

"A few. This is as far up as they go." I thought how the soil was too dry and not rocky enough in the higher land for live oaks. The pastures above supported an entirely different ecosystem than the valley with their thorny mesquite trees, prairie grasses, prickly pear cactus and holly-like agarita bushes. "But the good thing is that it's high and flat and out of the flood plain, yet within view of the Santa Clara."

"As soon as you clear it out."

"That's what this winter is for."

"So what's so special about this spot?" Michael leaned against an oak tree.

"It's where I'm going to build a house." I ran over to him and jumped up on a low limb that jutted out from the tree on which he was leaning. I climbed onto a sprawling limb that arched away from the highest rock. I lay my body fully along the thick branch, balancing with one hand on a lateral limb.

"I knew you'd end up living here some day. This is an incredible place for a house."

"Yeah, it's the best home site on the whole place. It's almost in the center and totally hidden from view." I hugged the limb I was lying on as if I were greeting my best friend. I pointed to a rock that formed an overhang below a flat one above. "I'm going to have a deck that extends out over those rocks."

Michael walked to where I was pointing. "Here?"

"Yeah, and it will curve around the house, tracing the line of rocks." I continued pointing to different areas, and Michael in turn stood in each imaginary room: the kitchen adjoining a huge living room with a fireplace, the master bedroom with a bathroom with a glass wall along a whirlpool tub. "And over there, next to the garage, behind the loft . . . ." Michael walked to where I was pointing, to the sunniest spot which faced southeast. "That's where we'll build your studio."

I looked down at Michael, who stood in the sun shielding his eyes with his hand as he tried to look at me through the oak's leafy branches. Abby stood next to him wagging her tail. Michael grinned, walked toward me and then started to climb the tree. I leaned forward so he could see my wide smile. And then I looked around and saw the land rise in all directions, lightly wooded pastureland as far as I could see, so full with the promise of the spring wildflowers to come. I hung my head over the branch that I was straddling and saw a large snail undulating along a slick rock in the shade, moving faster than I thought a snail could ever move. I threw my head back and laughed out loud at the sight and then closed my eyes as I felt the tree shake when Michael joined me out on my limb.